SCARY CLASSICS

SCARY CLASSICS

Stories from the
Greatest Horror Writers
of All Time

ROXBURY PARK

LOWELL HOUSE JUVENILE
LOS ANGELES

NTC/Contemporary Publishing Group

Published by Lowell House
A division of NTC/Contemporary Publishing Group, Inc.
4255 West Touhy Avenue
Lincolnwood (Chicago), Illinois 60712-1975 U.S.A.

OI-O2WC II,54

Lowell House books can be purchased at special discounts when ordered
in balk for premiums and special sales. Contact Department CS at the
following address:

NTC/Contemporary Publishing Group
4255 West Touhy Avenue
Lincolnwood, IL 60712-1975,
1-800-323-4900

01-02

ISBN: 0-7373-0438-3
Library of Congress Control Number: 00-133247
Roxbury Park is a division of NTC/Contemporary Publishing Group, Inc.

Managing Director and Publisher: Jack Artenstein
Editor in Chief, Roxbury Park Books: Michael Artenstein
Director of Publishing Services: Rena Copperman
Senior Editor: Maria Magallanes
Editorial Assistant: Nicole Monastirsky
Interior Design: Robert S. Tinnon Design
Cover Art: Michele Lanci-Altomare

Printed and bound in the United States of America
00 01 02 DHD 10 9 8 7 6 5 4 3 2 1

CONTENTS

INTRODUCTION

What makes a classic story "classic"? Is it the famous name of the author? Or maybe the famous name of a character? Does the story itself have to be well-known? Who decides which stories become classics?

Well, a famous author certainly helps a story become a classic. Glancing down the table of contents in this book, you might recognize names such as, Charles Dickens, or Jack London. Other writers, like G. K. Chesterton, Saki, and E. Nesbit, while household names in their day, are remembered more for the unforgettable stories they wrote. There must be something then, besides an author's popularity that makes a story classic.

Famous characters also contribute to a story's reputation as a classic. Sherlock Holmes and Tarzan make appearances in this compilation of tales. Father Brown, the hero of Chesterton's tale, once had a host of loyal followers all to himself. Oscar Wilde's ghost, Sir Simon de Canterville, likewise haunted thousands of readers. Most of the characters, though, will be strangers to you, as they were to me. Again, there must be more to a classic story than a famous character.

Perhaps certain types of stories are more likely to earn the title of classic. Readers have always enjoyed detective stories, and there are two such tales in this book. Sherlock Holmes' investigation of the Red-headed League and Father Brown's inquiry into the absence of Mr. Glass both fall into this suspenseful category. Adventure stories, too, have long entertained us with daring exploits, dangerous journeys, and hair-raising escapes. Tarzan's run-in with the lion, the capture of the oyster pirates, and the adventure that ends on the edge of a volcano crater introduce us to perilous situations and resourceful heroes. One of the most popular genres is the ghost story. Several supernatural tales lurk within these pages to thrill, chill, and captivate you. Vampires, goblins, werewolves, and 300-year-old ghosts all make haunting appearances.

This still does not explain the success of these particular scary stories. For many, a classic story is one that remains with them for a long while after they close the book. These stories deserve their classic reputations because they introduce us to people and places that we cannot easily forget. One day you may be crossing a lonely field at sunset and think to yourself, "This is just as Saki described it. I'd better hurry or I might run into Gabriel-Ernest." Or perhaps you will see a job advertised in the newspaper, a job that demands strange qualifications, and remind myself of "The Red-headed League." Classic stories have a knack of reappearing this way.

So who decides which stories are classics? Why, you do, of course.

THE LION
FROM JUNGLE TALES OF TARZAN

Edgar Rice Burroughs
(1875–1950)

EDGAR RICE BURROUGHS was born in Chicago,
Illinois to prominent businessman George Tyler
Burroughs and his wife Mary Evaline Burroughs.
The fifth of six children, Burroughs attended several
private schools and military academies. Upon grad-
uation, he joined the army and served in the 7th
Cavalry. After his brief career as a soldier, Burroughs
tried a number of jobs, including gold miner, rail-
road policeman, office manager, accountant, and
light bulb and candy salesman. He did not find
much success in any of these attempts, and consequently turned in desperation to writing at the age
of 35.

His first book, *Under the Moons of Mars* (also
called *A Princess of Mars*) was an immediate hit. He
wrote many more books starring John Carter, the
hero of *Under the Moons of Mars*, and began several
new series such as The Carson of Venus books, the
Pellucidar tales, and The Land That Time Forgot
trilogy. Burroughs introduced his most famous
character in 1912, when he published *Tarzan of the
Apes*. The demand for more tales of Tarzan grew and

1

grew, causing Burroughs to create 24 more books starring the lord of the jungle. In fact, Tarzan became so popular that the area of California where Burroughs settled was named Tarzana.

This tale comes from early in the life of Tarzan, before the young hero established his rule of the jungle. The vivid images and descriptions come entirely from Burrough's active imagination, for the author never visited Africa.

Numa, the lion, crouched behind a thorn bush close beside the drinking pool where the river eddied just below the bend. There was a ford there and on either bank a well-worn trail, broadened far out at the river's brim, where, for countless centuries, the wild things of the jungle and of the plains beyond had come down to drink, the carnivora with bold and fearless majesty, the herbivora timorous, hesitating, fearful.

Numa, the lion, was hungry, he was very hungry, and so he was quite silent now. On his way to the drinking place he had moaned often and roared not a little; but as he neared the spot where he would lie in wait for Bara, the deer, or Horta, the boar, or some other of the many luscious-fleshed creatures who came hither to drink, he was silent. It was a grim, terrible silence, shot through with yellow-green light of ferocious eyes, punctuated with undulating tremors of sinuous tail.

It was Pacco, the zebra, who came first, and Numa, the lion, could scarce restrain a roar of anger, for of all the plains people, none are more wary than Pacco, the zebra. Behind the black-striped stallion came a herd of 30 or 40 of the plump and vicious little horselike beasts. As he neared the river, the leader paused often, cocking his ears and raising his muzzle to sniff the gentle breeze for the tell-tale scent spoor of the dread flesh-eaters.

Numa shifted uneasily, drawing his hind quarters far beneath his tawny body, gathering himself for the sudden charge and the savage assault. His eyes shot hungry fire. His great muscles quivered to the excitement of the moment.

Pacco came a little nearer, halted, snorted, and wheeled. There was a pattering of scurrying hoofs and the herd was gone; but Numa, the lion, moved not. He was familiar with the ways of Pacco, the zebra. He knew that he would return, though many times he might wheel and fly before he summoned the courage to lead his harem and his offspring to the water. There was the chance that Pacco might be frightened off entirely. Numa had seen this happen before, and so he became almost rigid lest he be the one to send them galloping, waterless, back to the plain.

Again and again came Pacco and his family, and again and again did they turn and flee; but each time they came closer to the river, until at last the plump stallion dipped his velvet muzzle daintily into the water. The others, stepping warily, approached their leader. Numa selected a sleek, fat filly and his flaming eyes burned greedily as they feasted upon her, for Numa, the lion, loves scarce anything better than the meat of Pacco, perhaps because Pacco is, of all the grass-eaters, the most difficult to catch.

Slowly the lion rose, and as he rose, a twig snapped beneath one of his great, padded paws. Like a shot from a rifle he charged upon the filly; but the snapped twig had been enough to startle the timorous quarry, so that they were in instant flight simultaneously with Numa's charge.

The stallion was last, and with a prodigious leap, the lion catapulted through the air to seize him; but the snapping twig had robbed Numa of his dinner, though his mighty talons raked the zebra's glossy rump, leaving four crimson bars across the beautiful coat.

It was an angry Numa that quitted the river and prowled, fierce, dangerous, and hungry, into the jungle. Far from particular now was his appetite. Even Dango, the hyena, would have seemed a tidbit to that ravenous maw. And in this temper it was that the lion came upon the tribe of Kerchak, the great ape.

One does not look for Numa, the lion, this late in the morning. He should be lying up asleep beside his last night's kill by now; but Numa had made no kill last night. He was still hunting, hungrier than ever.

The anthropoids were idling about the clearing, the first keen desire of the morning's hunger having been satisfied. Numa scented them long before he saw them. Ordinarily he would have turned away in search of other game, for even Numa respected the mighty muscles and the sharp fangs of the great bulls of the tribe of Kerchak, but today he kept on steadily toward them, his bristled snout wrinkled into a savage snarl.

Without an instant's hesitation, Numa charged the moment he reached a point from where the apes were visible to him. There were a dozen or more of the hairy, manlike creatures upon the ground in a little glade. In a tree at one side sat a brown-skinned youth. He saw Numa's swift charge; he saw the apes turn and flee, huge bulls trampling upon little balus; only a single she held her ground to meet the charge, a young she inspired by new motherhood to the great sacrifice that her balu might escape.

Tarzan leaped from his perch, screaming at the flying bulls beneath and at those who squatted in the safety of surrounding trees. Had the bulls stood their ground, Numa would not have carried through that charge unless goaded by great rage or the gnawing pangs of starvation. Even then he would not have come off unscathed.

If the bulls heard, they were too slow in responding, for Numa had seized the mother ape and dragged her into the jungle before the males had sufficiently collected their wits and their courage to rally in defense of their fellow. Tarzan's angry voice aroused similar anger in the breasts of the apes. Snarling and barking they followed Numa into the dense labyrinth of foliage wherein he sought to hide himself from them. The ape-man was in the lead, moving rapidly and yet with caution, depending even more upon his ears and nose than upon his eyes for information of the lion's whereabouts.

The spoor was easy to follow, for the dragged body of the victim left a plain trail, blood-spattered and scentful. Even such dull creatures as you or I might easily have followed it. To Tarzan and the apes of Kerchak it was as obvious as a cement sidewalk.

Tarzan knew that they were nearing the great cat even before he heard an angry growl of warning just ahead. Calling to the apes to follow his example, he swung into a tree and a moment later Numa was surrounded by a ring of growling beasts, well out of reach of his fangs and talons but within plain sight of him. The carnivore crouched with his fore-quarters upon the she-ape. Tarzan could see that the latter was already dead; but something within him made it seem quite necessary to rescue the useless body from the clutches of the enemy and to punish him.

He shrieked taunts and insults at Numa, and tearing dead branches from the tree in which he danced, hurled them at the lion. The apes followed his example. Numa roared out in rage and vexation. He was hungry, but under such conditions he could not feed.

The apes, if they had been left to themselves, would doubtless soon have left the lion to peaceful enjoyment of his feast, for was not the she dead? They could not restore her to life by throwing sticks at Numa, and they might even now be feeding in quiet themselves; but Tarzan was of a different mind. Numa must be punished and driven away. He must be taught that even though he killed a Mangani, he would not be permitted to feed upon his kill. The man-mind looked into the future, while the apes perceived only the immediate present. They would be content to escape to-day the menace of Numa, while Tarzan saw the necessity, and the means as well, of safeguarding the days to come.

So he urged the great anthropoids on until Numa was showered with missiles that kept his head dodging and his voice pealing forth its savage protest; but still he clung desperately to his kill.

The twigs and branches hurled at Numa, Tarzan soon realized, did not hurt him greatly even when they struck him, and did not injure him at all, so the ape-man looked about for more effective missiles, nor did he have to look long. An out-cropping of decomposed granite not far from Numa suggested ammunition of a much more painful nature. Calling to the apes to watch him, Tarzan slipped to the ground and gathered a handful of small fragments. He knew that when once they had seen him carry out his idea they would be much quicker to follow his lead than to obey his instructions, were he to command them to procure pieces of rock and hurl them at Numa, for Tarzan was not then king of the apes of the tribe of Kerchak. That came in later years. Now he was but a youth, though one who already had wrested for himself a place in the councils of the savage beasts among whom a strange fate had cast him. The sullen bulls of the older generation still hated him as beasts hate those of whom they are suspicious, whose scent characteristic is the scent characteristic of an alien order and, therefore, of an enemy order. The younger bulls, those who had grown up through childhood as his playmates, were as accustomed to Tarzan's scent as to that of any other member of the tribe. They felt no greater suspicion of him than of any other bull of their acquaintance; yet they did not love him. They were a morose and peevish band at best, though here and there were those among them in whom germinated the primal seeds of humanity—reversions to type, these, doubtless; reversions to the ancient progenitor who took the first step out of ape-hood toward humanness, when he walked more often upon his hind feet and discovered other things for idle hands to do.

So now Tarzan led where he could not yet command. He had long since discovered the apish propensity for

mimicry and learned to make use of it. Having filled his arms with fragments of rotted granite, he clambered again into a tree, and it pleased him to see that the apes had followed his example.

During the brief respite while they were gathering their ammunition, Numa had settled himself to feed; but scarce had he arranged himself and his kill when a sharp piece of rock hurled by the practiced hand of the ape-man struck him upon the cheek. His sudden roar of pain and rage was smothered by a volley from the apes, who had seen Tarzan's act. Numa shook his massive head and glared upward at his tormentors. For a half hour they pursued him with rocks and broken branches, and though he dragged his kill into densest thickets, yet they always found a way to reach him with their missiles, giving him no opportunity to feed, and driving him on and on.

The hairless ape-thing with the man scent was worst of all, for he had even the temerity to advance upon the ground to within a few yards of the Lord of the Jungle, that he might with greater accuracy and force hurl the sharp bits of granite and the heavy sticks at him. Time and again did Numa charge—sudden, vicious charges—but the lithe, active tormentor always managed to elude him and with such insolent ease that the lion forgot even his great hunger in the consuming passion of his rage, leaving his meat for considerable spaces of time in vain efforts to catch his enemy.

The apes and Tarzan pursued the great beast to a natural clearing, where Numa evidently determined to make a last stand, taking up his position in the center of the open space, which was far enough from any tree to render him practically immune from the rather erratic throwing of the apes, though Tarzan still found him with most persistent and aggravating frequency.

This, however, did not suit the ape-man, since Numa now suffered an occasional missile with no more than a snarl, while he settled himself to partake of his delayed feast. Tarzan scratched his head, pondering some more effective method of offense, for he had determined to prevent Numa from profiting in any way through his attack upon the tribe.

The man-mind reasoned against the future, while the shaggy apes thought only of their present hatred of this ancestral enemy. Tarzan guessed that should Numa find it an easy thing to snatch a meal from the tribe of Kerchak, it would be but a short time before their existence would be one living nightmare of hideous watchfulness and dread. Numa must be taught that the killing of an ape brought immediate punishment and no rewards. It would take but a few lessons to insure the former safety of the tribe. This must be some old lion whose failing strength and agility had forced him to any prey that he could catch; but even a single lion, undisputed, could exterminate the tribe, or at least make its existence so precarious and so terrifying that life would no longer be a pleasant condition.

"Let him hunt among the Gomangani," thought Tarzan. "He will find them easier prey. I will teach ferocious Numa that he may not hunt the Mangani."

But how to wrest the body of his victim from the feeding lion was the first question to be solved. At last Tarzan hit upon a plan. To anyone but Tarzan of the Apes it might have seemed rather a risky plan, and perhaps it did even to him; but Tarzan rather liked things that contained a considerable element of danger. At any rate, I rather doubt that you or I would have chosen a similar plan for foiling an angry and a hungry lion.

Tarzan required assistance in the scheme he had hit upon and his assistant must be equally as brave and almost as active as he. The ape-man's eyes fell upon Taug, the playmate of his childhood, the rival in his first love and now, of all the bulls of the tribe, the only one that might be thought to hold in his savage brain any such feeling toward Tarzan as we describe among ourselves as friendship. At least, Tarzan knew, Taug was courageous, and he was young and agile and wonderfully muscled.

"Taug!" cried the ape-man. The great ape looked up from a dead limb he was attempting to tear from a lightning-blasted tree. "Go close to Numa and worry him," said Tarzan. "Worry him until he charges. Lead him away from the body of Mamka. Keep him away as long as you can."

Taug nodded. He was across the clearing from Tarzan. Wresting the limb at last from the tree he dropped to the ground and advanced toward Numa, growling and barking out his insults. The worried lion looked up and rose to his feet. His tail went stiffly erect and Taug turned in flight, for he knew that warning signal of the charge.

From behind the lion, Tarzan ran quickly toward the center of the clearing and the body of Mamka. Numa, all his eyes for Taug, did not see the ape-man. Instead he shot forward after the fleeing bull, who had turned in flight not an instant too soon, since he reached the nearest tree but a yard or two ahead of the pursuing demon. Like a cat the heavy anthropoid scampered up the bole of his sanctuary. Numa's talons missed him by little more than inches.

For a moment the lion paused beneath the tree, glaring up at the ape and roaring until the earth trembled, then he turned back again toward his kill, and as he did so, his tail shot once more to rigid erectness and he charged back even more ferociously than he had come, for what he saw was the naked man-thing running toward the farther trees with the bloody carcass of his prey across a giant shoulder.

The apes, watching the grim race from the safety of the trees, screamed taunts at Numa and warnings to Tarzan. The high sun, hot and brilliant, fell like a spotlight upon the actors in the little clearing, portraying them in glaring relief to the audience in the leafy shadows of the surrounding trees. The light-brown body of the naked youth, all but hidden by the shaggy carcass of the killed ape, the red blood streaking his smooth hide, his muscles rolling, velvety, beneath. Behind him the black-maned lion, head flattened, tail extended, racing, a jungle thoroughbred, across the sunlit clearing.

Ah, but this was life! With death at his heels, Tarzan thrilled with the joy of such living as this; but would he reach the trees ahead of the rampant death so close behind?

Gunto swung from a limb in a tree before him. Gunto was screaming warnings and advice.

"Catch me!" cried Tarzan, and with his heavy burden leaped straight for the big bull hanging there by his hind feet and one forepaw. And Gunto caught them—the big ape-man and the dead weight of the slain she-ape—caught them with one great, hairy paw and whirled them upward until Tarzan's fingers closed upon a near-by branch.

Beneath, Numa leaped; but Gunto, heavy and awkward as he may have appeared, was as quick as Manu, the monkey, so that the lion's talons but barely grazed him, scratching a bloody streak beneath one hairy arm.

Tarzan carried Mamka's corpse to a high crotch, where even Sheeta, the panther, could not get it. Numa paced angrily back and forth beneath the tree, roaring frightfully. He had been robbed of his kill and his revenge also. He was very savage indeed; but his despoilers were well out of his reach, and after hurling a few taunts and missiles at him they swung away through the trees, fiercely reviling him.

Tarzan thought much upon the little adventure of that day. He foresaw what might happen should the great carnivora of the jungle turn their serious attention upon the tribe of Kerchak, the great ape, but equally he thought upon the wild scramble of the apes for safety when Numa first charged among them. There is little humor in the jungle that is not grim and awful. The beasts have little or no conception of humor; but the young Englishman saw humor in many things which presented no humorous angle to his associates.

Since earliest childhood he had been a searcher after fun, much to the sorrow of his fellow-apes, and now he saw the humor of the frightened panic of the apes and the baffled rage of Numa even in this grim jungle adventure which had robbed Mamka of life, and jeopardized that of many members of the tribe.

It was but a few weeks later that Sheeta, the panther, made a sudden rush among the tribe and snatched a little balu from a tree where it had been hidden while its mother sought food. Sheeta got away with his small prize unmolested. Tarzan was very wroth. He spoke to the bulls of the ease with which Numa and Sheeta, in a single moon, had slain two members of the tribe.

"They will take us all for food," he cried. "We hunt as we will through the jungle, paying no heed to approaching enemies. Even Manu, the monkey, does not so. He keeps two or three always watching for enemies. Pacco, the zebra, and Wappi, the antelope, have those about the herd who keep watch while the others feed, while we, the great Mangani, let Numa, and Sabor, and Sheeta come when they will and carry us off to feed their balus.

"Gr-r-rmph," said Numgo.

"What are we to do?" asked Taug.

"We, too, should have two or three always watching for the approach of Numa, and Sabor, and Sheeta," replied Tarzan. "No others need we fear, except Histah, the snake, and if we watch for the others we will see Histah if he comes, though gliding ever so silently."

And so it was that the great apes of the tribe of Kerchak posted sentries thereafter, who watched upon three sides while the tribe hunted, scattered less than had been their wont.

But Tarzan went abroad alone, for Tarzan was a man-thing and sought amusement and adventure and such humor as the grim and terrible jungle offers to those who know it and do not fear it—a weird humor shot with blazing eyes and dappled with the crimson of lifeblood. While others sought only food and love, Tarzan of the Apes sought food and joy.

One day he hovered above the palisaded village of Mbonga, the chief, the jet cannibal of the jungle primeval. He saw, as he had seen many times before, the witch-doctor,

Rabba Kega, decked out in the head and hide of Gorgo, the buffalo. It amused Tarzan to see a Gomangani parading as Gorgo; but it suggested nothing in particular to him until he chanced to see stretched against the side of Mbonga's hut the skin of a lion with the head still on. Then a broad grin widened the handsome face of the savage beast-youth.

Back into the jungle he went until chance, agility, strength, and cunning backed by his marvelous powers of perception, gave him an easy meal. If Tarzan felt that the world owed him a living he also realized that it was for him to collect it, nor was there ever a better collector than this son of an English lord, who knew even less of the ways of his forbears than he did of the forbears themselves, which was nothing.

It was quite dark when Tarzan returned to the village of Mbonga and took his now polished perch in the tree which overhangs the palisade upon one side of the walled enclosure. As there was nothing in particular to feast upon in the village there was little life in the single street, for only an orgy of flesh and native beer could draw out the people of Mbonga. Tonight they sat gossiping about their cooking fires, the older members of the tribe; or, if they were young, paired off in the shadows cast by the palm-thatched huts.

Tarzan dropped lightly into the village, and sneaking stealthily in the concealment of the denser shadows, approached the hut of the chief, Mbonga. Here he found that which he sought. There were warriors all about him; but they did not know that the feared devil-god slunk noiselessly so near them, nor did they see him possess himself of that which he coveted and depart from their village as noiselessly as he had come.

Later that night, as Tarzan curled himself for sleep, he lay for a long time looking up at the burning planets and the twinkling stars and at Goro the moon, and he smiled. He recalled how ludicrous the great bulls had appeared in their mad scramble for safety that day when Numa had charged among them and seized Mamka, and yet he knew them to be fierce and courageous. It was the sudden shock of surprise that always sent them into a panic; but of this Tarzan was not as yet fully aware. That was something he was to learn in the near future.

He fell asleep with a broad grin upon his face.

Manu, the monkey, awoke him in the morning by dropping discarded bean pods upon his upturned face from a branch a short distance above him. Tarzan looked up and smiled. He had been awakened thus before many times. He and Manu were fairly good friends, their friendship operating upon a reciprocal basis. Sometimes Manu would come running early in the morning to awaken Tarzan and tell him that Bara, the deer, was feeding close at hand, or that Horta, the boar, was asleep in a mudhole hard by, and in return Tarzan broke open the shells of the harder nuts and fruits for Manu, or frightened away Histah, the snake.

The sun had been up for some time, and the tribe had already wandered off in search of food. Manu indicated the direction they had taken with a wave of his hand and a few piping notes of his squeaky little voice.

"Come, Manu," said Tarzan, "and you will see that which shall make you dance for joy and squeal your wrinkled little head off. Come, follow Tarzan of the Apes."

With that he set off in the direction Manu had indicated and above him, chattering, scolding and squealing, skipped Manu, the monkey. Across Tarzan's shoulders was the thing he had stolen from the village of Mbonga, the chief, the evening before.

The tribe was feeding in the forest beside the clearing where Gunto, and Taug, and Tarzan had so harassed Numa and finally taken away from him the fruit of his kill. Some of them were in the clearing itself. In peace and content they fed, for were there not three sentries, each watching upon a different side of the herd? Tarzan had taught them this, and though he had been away for several days hunting alone, as he often did, or visiting at the cabin by the sea, they had not as yet forgotten his admonitions, and if they continued for a short time longer to post sentries, it would become a habit of their tribal life and thus be perpetuated indefinitely.

But Tarzan, who knew them better than they knew them-selves, was confident that they had ceased to place the watch-ers about them the moment that he had left them, and now he planned not only to have a little fun at their expense but to teach them a lesson in preparedness, which, by the way, is even a more vital issue in the jungle than in civilized places. That you and I exist today must be due to the preparedness of some shaggy anthropoid of the Oligocene. Of course the apes of Kerchak were always prepared, after their own way—Tarzan had merely suggested a new and additional safeguard.

Gunto was posted today to the north of the clearing. He squatted in the fork of a tree from where he might view the jungle for quite a distance about him. It was he who first discovered the enemy. A rustling in the undergrowth attracted his attention, and a moment later he had a partial view of a shaggy mane and tawny yellow back. Just a glimpse it was through the matted foliage beneath him; but it brought from Gunto's leathern lungs a shrill "Kreeg-ah!" which is the ape for beware, or danger.

Instantly the tribe took up the cry until "Kreeg-ahs!" rang through the jungle about the clearing as apes swung quickly to places of safety among the lower branches of the trees and the great bulls hastened in the direction of Gunto.

And then into the clearing strode Numa, the lion— majestic and mighty, and from a deep chest issued the moan and the cough and the rumbling roar that set stiff hairs to bristling from shaggy craniums down the length of mighty spines.

Inside the clearing, Numa paused and on the instant there fell upon him from the trees near by a shower of broken rock and dead limbs torn from age-old trees. A dozen times he was hit, and then the apes ran down and gathered other rocks, pelting him unmercifully.

Numa turned to flee, but his way was barred by a fusillade of sharp-cornered missiles, and then, upon the edge of the clearing, great Taug met him with a huge fragment of rock as large as a man's head, and down went the Lord of the Jungle beneath the stunning blow.

With shrieks and roars and loud barkings the great apes of the tribe of Kerchak rushed upon the fallen lion. Sticks and stones and yellow fangs menaced the still form. In another moment, before he could regain consciousness, Numa would be battered and torn until only a bloody mass of broken bones and matted hair remained of what had once been the most dreaded of jungle creatures.

But even as the sticks and stones were raised above him and the great fangs bared to tear him, there descended like a plummet from the trees above a diminutive figure with long, white whiskers and a wrinkled face. Square upon the body of Numa it alighted and there it danced and screamed and shrieked out its challenge against the bulls of Kerchak.

For an instant they paused, paralyzed by the wonder of the thing. It was Manu, the monkey, Manu, the little coward, and here he was daring the ferocity of the great Mangani, hopping about upon the carcass of Numa, the lion, and crying out that they must not strike it again.

And when the bulls paused, Manu reached down and seized a tawny ear. With all his little might he tugged upon the heavy head until slowly it turned back, revealing the tousled, black head and clean-cut profile of Tarzan of the Apes.

Some of the older apes were for finishing what they had commenced; but Taug, sullen, mighty Taug, sprang quickly to the ape-man's side and straddling the unconscious form warned back those who would have struck his childhood playmate. And Teeka, his mate, came too, taking her place with bared fangs at Taug's side. Others followed their example, until at last Tarzan was surrounded by a ring of hairy champions who would permit no enemy to approach him.

It was a surprised and chastened Tarzan who opened his eyes to consciousness a few minutes later. He looked about him at the surrounding apes and slowly there returned to him a realization of what had occurred.

Gradually a broad grin illuminated his features. His

bruises were many and they hurt; but the good that had come from his adventure was worth all that it had cost. He had learned, for instance, that the apes of Kerchak had heeded his teaching, and he had learned that he had good friends among the sullen beasts whom he had thought without sentiment. He had discovered that Manu, the monkey—even little, cowardly Manu—had risked his life in his defense.

It made Tarzan very glad to know these things; but at the other lesson he had been taught he reddened. He had always been a joker, the only joker in the grim and terrible company; but now as he lay there half dead from his hurts, he almost swore a solemn oath forever to forego practical joking—almost; but not quite.

THE

RED-HEADED LEAGUE
Sir Arthur Conan Doyle
(1859–1930)

ARTHUR CONAN DOYLE, born in Scotland on May 22nd, 1859, was one of ten children, whose family traced their ancestors all the way back to the Plantagenet line of kings. All the Doyle children grew up to be quite talented, and Arthur was no exception. After finishing school, Conan Doyle earned a medical degree at Edinburgh University, where he found inspiration for many of his later characters, including Professor George Edward Challenger of *The Lost World.*

At Edinburgh, Conan Doyle also discovered the model for his most famous character, Dr. Joseph Bell, whose remarkable deductions about the history of his patients suggested the scientific logic of Sherlock Holmes. Conan Doyle himself probably served as the model for Dr. Watson, the reliable companion to the famous detective.

In addition to the four books and numerous short stories about Holmes, Conan Doyle also wrote a number of historical novels, including *The White Company, Sir Nigel, Micah Clarke*, and *The Great Shadow.* He also worked as a war correspondent, ran for political office, investigated a few unusual court cases, played a number of sports, and became something of an expert at early photography.

I had called upon my friend, Mr. Sherlock Holmes, one day in the autumn of last year and found him in deep conversation with a very stout, florid-faced, elderly gentleman with fiery red hair. With an apology for my intrusion, I was about to withdraw when Holmes pulled me abruptly into the room and closed the door behind me.

"You could not possibly have come at a better time, my dear Watson," he said cordially.

"I was afraid that you were engaged."

"So I am. Very much so."

"Then I can wait in the next room."

"Not at all. This gentleman, Mr. Wilson, has been my partner and helper in many of my most successful cases, and I have no doubt that he will be of the utmost use to me in yours also."

The stout gentleman half rose from his chair and gave a bob of greeting, with a quick little questioning glance from his small fat-encircled eyes.

"Try the settee," said Holmes, relapsing into his armchair and putting his fingertips together, as was his custom when in judicial moods. "I know, my dear Watson, that you share my love of all that is bizarre and outside the conventions and humdrum routine of everyday life. You have shown your relish for it by the enthusiasm which has prompted you to chronicle, and, if you will excuse my saying so, somewhat to embellish so many of my own little adventures."

"Your cases have indeed been of the greatest interest to me," I observed.

"You will remember that I remarked the other day, just before we went into the very simple problem presented by Miss Mary Sutherland, that for strange effects and extraordinary combinations we must go to life itself, which is always far more daring than any effort of the imagination."

"A proposition which I took the liberty of doubting."

"You did, Doctor, but none the less you must come round to my view, for otherwise I shall keep on piling fact upon fact on you until your reason breaks down under them and acknowledges me to be right. Now, Mr. Jabez Wilson here has been good enough to call upon me this morning, and to begin a narrative which promises to be one of the most singular which I have listened to for some time. You have heard me remark that the strangest and most unique things are very often connected not with the larger but with the smaller crimes, and occasionally, indeed, where there is room for doubt whether any positive crime has been committed. As far as I have heard it is impossible for me to say whether the present case is an instance of crime or not, but the course of events is certainly among the most singular that I have ever listened to. Perhaps, Mr. Wilson, you would have the great kindness to recommence your narrative. I ask you not merely because my friend Dr. Watson has not heard the opening part but also because the peculiar nature of the story makes me anxious to have every possible detail from your lips. As a rule, when I have heard some slight indication of the course of events, I am able to guide myself by the thousands of other similar cases which occur to my memory. In the present instance I am forced to admit that the facts are, to the best of my belief, unique."

The portly client puffed out his chest with an appearance of some little pride and pulled a dirty and wrinkled newspaper from the inside pocket of his greatcoat. As he glanced down the advertisement column, with his head thrust forward and the paper flattened out upon his knee, I took a good look at the man and endeavored, after the fashion of my companion, to read the indications which might be presented by his dress or appearance. I did not gain very much, however, by my inspection.

Our visitor bore every mark of being an average commonplace British tradesman, obese, pompous, and slow. He wore rather baggy gray shepherd's check trousers, a not over-clean black frock-coat, unbuttoned in the front, and a drab waistcoat with a heavy brassy Albert chain, and a square pierced bit of metal dangling down as an ornament. A frayed top-hat and a faded brown overcoat with a wrinkled velvet collar lay upon a chair beside him. Altogether, look as I would, there was nothing remarkable about the man save his blazing red head, and the expression of extreme chagrin and discontent upon his features.

Sherlock Holmes's quick eye took in my occupation, and he shook his head with a smile as he noticed my questioning glances. "Beyond the obvious facts that he has at some time done manual labor, that he takes snuff, that he is a Freemason, that he has been in China, and that he has done a considerable amount of writing lately, I can deduce nothing else."

Mr. Jabez Wilson started up in his chair, with his fore-finger upon the paper, but his eyes upon my companion.

"How, in the name of good-fortune, did you know all that, Mr. Holmes?" he asked. "How did you know, for example, that I did manual labor? It's as true as gospel, for I began as a ship's carpenter."

"Your hands, my dear sir. Your right hand is quite a size larger than your left. You have worked with it, and the muscles are more developed."

"Well, the snuff, then, and the Freemasonry?"

"I won't insult your intelligence by telling you how I read that, especially as, rather against the strict rules of your order, you use an arc-and-compass breastpin."

"Ah, of course, I forgot that. But the writing?"

"What else can be indicated by that right cuff so very shiny for five inches, and the left one with the smooth patch near the elbow where you rest it upon the desk?"

"Well, but China?" "The fish that you have tattooed immediately above your right wrist could only have been done in China. I have made a small study of tattoo marks and have even contributed to the literature of the subject. That trick of staining the fishes' scales of a delicate pink is quite peculiar to China. When, in addition, I see a Chinese coin hanging from your watch-chain, the matter becomes even more simple."

Mr. Jabez Wilson laughed heavily. "Well, I never!" said he. "I thought at first that you had done something clever, but I see that there was nothing in it, after all."

"I begin to think, Watson," said Holmes, "that I make a mistake in explaining. *Omne ignotum pro magnifico*, you know, and my poor little reputation, such as it is, will suffer shipwreck if I am so candid. Can you not find the advertisement, Mr. Wilson?"

"Yes, I have got it now," he answered with his thick red finger planted halfway down the column. "Here it is. This is what began it all. You just read it for yourself, sir."

I took the paper from him and read as follows.

TO THE RED-HEADED LEAGUE:

On account of the bequest of the late Ezekiah Hopkins, of Lebanon, Pennsylvania, U.S.A., there is now another vacancy open which entitles a member of the League to a salary of four pounds a week for purely nominal services. All red-headed men who are sound in body and mind and above the age of 21 years, are eligible. Apply in person on Monday, at 11 o'clock, to Duncan Ross, at the offices of the League, 7 Pope's Court, Fleet Street.

"What on earth does this mean?" I announced after I had twice read over the extraordinary announcement.

Holmes chuckled and wriggled in his chair, as was his habit when in high spirits. "It is a little off the beaten track, isn't it?" said he. "And now, Mr. Wilson, off you go at scratch and tell us all about yourself, your household, and the effect which this advertisement had upon your fortunes. You will first make a note, Doctor, of the paper and the date."

"It is *The Morning Chronicle* of April 27, 1890. Just two months ago."

"Very good. Now, Mr. Wilson?"

"Well, it is just as I have been telling you, Mr. Sherlock Holmes," said Jabez Wilson, mopping his forehead; "I have a small pawnbroker's business at Coburg Square, near the City. It's not a very large affair, and of late years it has not done more than just give me a living. I used to be able to keep two assistants, but now I only keep one; and I would have a job to pay him but that he is willing to come for half wages so as to learn the business."

"What is the name of this obliging youth?" asked Sherlock Holmes.

"His name is Vincent Spaulding, and he's not such a youth, either. It's hard to say his age. I should not wish a smarter assistant, Mr. Holmes; and I know very well that he could better himself and earn twice what I am able to give him. But, after all, if he is satisfied, why should I put ideas in his head?"

"Why, indeed? You seem most fortunate in having an employee who comes under the full market price. It is not a common experience among employers in this age. I don't know that your assistant is not as remarkable as your advertisement."

"Oh, he has his faults, too," said Mr. Wilson. "Never was such a fellow for photography. Snapping away with a camera when he ought to be improving his mind, and then diving down into the cellar like a rabbit into its hole to develop his pictures. That is his main fault, but on the whole he's a good worker. There's no vice in him."

"He is still with you, I presume?"

"Yes, sir. He and a girl of 14, who does a bit of simple cooking and keeps the place clean—that's all I have in the house, for I am a widower and never had any family. We live very quietly, sir, the three of us; and we keep a roof over our heads and pay our debts, if we do nothing more.

"The first thing that put us out was that advertisement. Spaulding, he came down into the office just this day eight weeks, with this very paper in his hand, and he says:

"'I wish to the Lord, Mr. Wilson, that I was a red-headed man.'

"'Why that?' I asks.

"'Why,' says he, 'here's another vacancy on the League of the Red-headed Men. It's worth quite a little fortune to any man who gets it, and I understand that there are more vacancies than there are men, so that the trustees are at their wits' end what to do with the money. If my hair would only change color, here's a nice little crib all ready for me to step into.'

"'Why, what is it, then?' I asked. You see. Mr. Holmes, I am a very stay-at-home man, and as my business came to me instead of my having to go to it, I was often weeks on end without putting my foot over the door-mat. In that way I didn't know much of what was going on outside, and I was always glad of a bit of news.

"'Have you never heard of the League of the Red-headed Men?' he asked with his eyes open.

"'Never.'

"'Why, I wonder at that, for you are eligible yourself for one of the vacancies.'

"'And what are they worth?' I asked.

"'Oh, merely a couple of hundred a year, but the work is slight, and it need not interfere very much with one's other occupations.'

"Well, you can easily think that that made me prick up my ears, for the business has not been over-good for some years, and an extra couple of hundred would have been very handy.

"'Tell me all about it,' said I.

"'Well' said he, showing me the advertisement, 'you can see for yourself that the League has a vacancy, and there is the address where you should apply for particulars. As far as I can make out, the League was founded by an American millionaire, Ezekiah Hopkins, who was very peculiar in his ways. He was himself red-headed, and he had a great sympathy for all red-headed men; so when he died it was found that he had left his enormous fortune in the hands of trustees, with instructions to apply the interest to the providing of easy berths to men whose hair is of that color. From all I hear it is splendid pay and very little to do.'

"'But,' said I, 'there would be millions of red-headed men who would apply.'

"'Not so many as you might think,' he answered. 'You see it is really confined to Londoners, and to grown men. This American had started from London when he was young, and he wanted to do the old town a good turn. Then, again, I have heard it is no use your applying if your hair is light red, or dark red, or anything but real bright, blazing, fiery red. Now, if you cared to apply, Mr. Wilson, you would just walk in; but perhaps it would hardly be worth your while to put yourself out of the way for the sake of a few hundred pounds.'

"Now, it is a fact, gentlemen, as you may see for yourselves, that my hair is of a very full and rich tint, so that it seemed to me that if there was to be any competition in the matter I stood as good a chance as any man that I had ever met. Vincent Spaulding seemed to know so much about it that I thought he might prove useful, so I just ordered him to put up the shutters for the day and to come right away with me. He was very willing to have a holiday, so we shut the business up and started off for the address that was given us in the advertisement.

"I never hope to see such a sight as that again, Mr. Holmes. From north, south, east, and west every man who had a shade of red in his hair had tramped into the city to answer the advertisement. Fleet Street was choked with red-headed folk, and Pope's Court looked like a coster's orange barrow. I should not have thought there were so many in the whole country as were brought together by that single advertisement. Every shade of color they were—straw, lemon, orange, brick, Irish-setter, liver, clay; but, as Spaulding said, there were not many who had the real vivid flame-colored tint. When I saw how many were waiting, I would have given it up in despair; but Spaulding would not hear of it. How he did it I could not imagine, but he pushed and pulled and butted until he got me through the crowd, and right up to the steps which led to the office. There was a double stream upon the stair, some going up in hope, and some coming back dejected; but we wedged in as well as we could and soon found ourselves in the office."

"Your experience has been a most entertaining one," remarked Holmes as his client paused and refreshed his memory with a huge pinch of snuff. "Pray continue your very interesting statement."

"There was nothing in the office but a couple of wooden chairs and a deal table, behind which sat a small man with a head that was even redder than mine. He said a few words to each candidate as he came up, and then he always managed to find some fault in them which would disqualify them. Getting a vacancy did not seem to be such a very easy matter, after all. However, when our turn came the little man was much more favorable to me than to any of the others, and he closed the door as we entered, so that he might have a private word with us.

"'This is Mr. Jabez Wilson,' said my assistant, 'and he is willing to fill a vacancy in the League.'

"'And he is admirably suited for it,' the other answered. 'He has every requirement. I cannot recall when I have seen anything so fine.' He took a step backward, cocked his head on one side, and gazed at my hair until I felt quite bashful. Then suddenly he plunged forward, wrung my hand, and congratulated me warmly on my success.

"'It would be injustice to hesitate,' said he. 'You will, however, I am sure, excuse me for taking an obvious precaution.' With that he seized my hair in both his hands, and tugged until I yelled with the pain. 'There is water in your eyes,' said he as he released me. 'I perceive that all is as it should be. But we have to be careful, for we have twice been deceived by wigs and once by paint. I could tell you tales of cobbler's wax which would disgust you with human nature.'

He stepped over to the window and shouted through it at the top of his voice that the vacancy was filled. A groan of disappointment came up from below, and the folk all trooped away in different directions until there was not a red-head to be seen except my own and that of the manager.

"'My name,' said he, 'is Mr. Duncan Ross, and I am myself one of the pensioners upon the fund left by our noble benefactor. Are you a married man, Mr. Wilson? Have you a family?'

"I answered that I had not.

"His face fell immediately.

"'Dear me!' he said gravely, 'that is very serious indeed! I am sorry to hear you say that. The fund was, of course, for the propagation and spread of the red-heads as well as for their maintenance. It is exceedingly unfortunate that you should be a bachelor.'

"My face lengthened at this, Mr. Holmes, for I thought that I was not to have the vacancy after all; but after thinking it over for a few minutes he said that it would be all right.

"'In the case of another,' said he, 'the objection might be fatal, but we must stretch a point in favor of a man with such a head of hair as yours. When shall you be able to enter upon your new duties?'

"'Well, it is a little awkward, for I have a business already,' said I.

"'Oh, never mind about that, Mr. Wilson!' said Vincent Spaulding. 'I should be able to look after that for you.'

"'What would be the hours?' I asked.

"'Ten to two.'

"Now a pawnbroker's business is mostly done of an evening, Mr. Holmes, especially Thursday and Friday evening, which is just before pay-day; so it would suit me very well to earn a little in the mornings. Besides, I knew that my assistant was a good man, and that he would see to anything that turned up.

"'That would suit me very well,' said I. 'And the pay?'

"'Is four pounds a week.'

"'And the work?'

"'Is purely nominal.'

"'What do you call purely nominal?'

"'Well, you have to be in the office, or at least in the building, the whole time. If you leave, you forfeit your whole position forever. The will is very clear upon that point. You don't comply with the conditions if you budge from the office during that time.'

"'It's only four hours a day, and I should not think of leaving,' said I.

"'No excuse will avail,' said Mr. Duncan Ross; 'neither sickness nor business nor anything else. There you must stay, or you lose your billet.'

"'And the work?'

"'Is to copy out the *Encyclopedia Britannica*. There is the first volume of it in that press. You must find your own ink, pens, and blotting-paper, but we provide this table and chair. Will you be ready tomorrow?'

"'Certainly,' I answered.

"'Then, good-bye, Mr. Jabez Wilson, and let me congratulate you once more on the important position which you have been fortunate enough to gain.' He bowed me out of the room and I went home with my assistant, hardly knowing what to say or do, I was so pleased at my own good fortune.

"Well, I thought over the matter all day, and by evening I was in low spirits again; for I had quite persuaded myself that the whole affair must be some great hoax or fraud, though what its object might be I could not imagine. It seemed altogether past belief that anyone could make such a will, or that they would pay such a sum for doing anything so simple as copying out the *Encyclopedia Britannica*. Vincent Spaulding did what he could to cheer me up, but by bedtime I had reasoned myself out of the whole thing. However, in the morning I determined to have a look at it anyhow, so I bought a penny bottle of ink, and with a quill-pen, and seven sheets of foolscap paper, I started off for Pope's Court.

"Well, to my surprise and delight, everything was as right as possible. The table was set out ready for me, and Mr. Duncan Ross was there to see that I got fairly to work. He started me off upon the letter A, and then he left me; but he would drop in from time to time to see that all was right with me. At two o'clock he bade me good-day, complimented me upon the amount that I had written, and locked the door of the office after me.

"This went on day after day, Mr. Holmes, and on Saturday the manager came in and planked down four golden sovereigns for my week's work. It was the same next week, and the same the week after. Every morning I was there at ten, and every afternoon I left at two. By degrees Mr. Duncan Ross took to coming in only once of a morning, and then, after a time, he did not come in at all. Still, of course, I never dared to leave the room for an instant, for I was not sure when he might come, and the billet was such a good one, and suited me so well, that I would not risk the loss of it.

"Eight weeks passed away like this, and I had written about Abbots and Archery and Armor and Architecture and Attica, and hoped with diligence that I might get on to the B's before very long. It cost me something in foolscap, and I had pretty nearly filled a shelf with my writings. And then suddenly the whole business came to an end."

"To an end?"

"Yes, sir. And no later than this morning. I went to my work as usual at ten o'clock, but the door was shut and locked, with a little square of card-board hammered on to the middle of the panel with a tack. Here it is, and you can read for yourself."

He held up a piece of white card-board about the size of a sheet of note-paper. It read in this fashion:

THE RED-HEADED LEAGUE IS DISSOLVED.

OCTOBER 9, 1890.

Sherlock Holmes and I surveyed this curt announcement and the rueful face behind it, until the comical side of the affair so completely overtopped every other consideration that we both burst out into a roar of laughter.

"I cannot see that there is anything very funny," cried our client, flushing up to the roots of his flaming head. "If you can do nothing better than laugh at me, I can go elsewhere."

"No, no," cried Holmes, shoving him back into the chair from which he had half risen. "I really wouldn't miss your case for the world. It is most refreshingly unusual. But there is, if you will excuse my saying so, something just a little funny about it. Pray what steps did you take when you found the card upon the door?"

"I was staggered, sir. I did not know what to do. Then I called at the offices round, but none of them seemed to know anything about it. Finally, I went to the landlord, who is an accountant living on the ground-floor, and I asked him if he could tell me what had become of the Red-headed League. He said that he had never heard of any such body. Then I asked him who Mr. Duncan Ross was. He answered that the name was new to him.

"'Well,' said I, 'the gentleman at No. 4.'

"'What, the red-headed man?'

"'Yes.'

"'Oh,' said he, 'his name was William Morris. He was a solicitor and was using my room as a temporary convenience until his new premises were ready. He moved out yesterday.'

"'Where could I find him?'

"'Oh, at his new offices. He did tell me the address. Yes, 17 King Edward Street, near St. Paul's.'

"I started off, Mr. Holmes, but when I got to that address it was a manufactory of artificial knee-caps, and no one in it had ever heard of either Mr. William Morris or Mr. Duncan Ross."

"And what did you do then?" asked Holmes.

"I went home to Saxe-Coburg Square, and I took the advice of my assistant. But he could not help me in any way. He could only say that if I waited I should hear by post. But that was not quite good enough, Mr. Holmes. I did not wish to lose such a place without a struggle, so, as I had heard that you were good enough to give advice to poor folk who were in need of it, I came right away to you."

"And you did very wisely," said Holmes. "Your case is an exceedingly remarkable one, and I shall be happy to look into it. From what you have told me I think that it is possible that graver issues hang from it than might at first sight appear."

"Grave enough!" said Mr. Jabez Wilson. "Why, I have lost four pound a week."

"As far as you are personally concerned," remarked Holmes, "I do not see that you have any grievance against this extraordinary league. On the contrary, you are, as I understand, richer by some 30 pounds, to say nothing of the minute knowledge which you have gained on every subject which comes under the letter A. You have lost nothing by them."

"No, sir. But I want to find out about them, and who they are, and what their object was in playing this prank— if it was a prank—upon me. It was a pretty expensive joke for them, for it cost them two and thirty pounds."

"We shall endeavor to clear up these points for you. And, first, one or two questions, Mr. Wilson. This assistant of yours who first called your attention to the advertisement— how long had he been with you?"

"About a month then."

"How did he come?"

"In answer to an advertisement."

"Was he the only applicant?"

"No, I had a dozen."

"Why did you pick him?"

"Because he was handy and would come cheap."

"At half-wages, in fact."

"Yes."

"What is he like, this Vincent Spaulding?"

"Small, stout-built, very quick in his ways, no hair on his face, though he's not short of thirty. Has a white splash of acid upon his forehead."

Holmes sat up in his chair in considerable excitement. "I thought as much," said he. "Have you ever observed that his ears are pierced for earrings?"

"Yes, sir. He told me that a gypsy had done it for him when he was a lad."

"Hum!" said Holmes, sinking back in deep thought. "He is still with you?"

"Oh, yes, sir; I have only just left him."

"And has your business been attended to in your absence?"

"Nothing to complain of, sir. There's never very much to do of a morning."

"That will do, Mr. Wilson. I shall be happy to give you an opinion upon the subject in the course of a day or two. Today is Saturday, and I hope that by Monday we may come to a conclusion."

"Well, Watson," said Holmes when our visitor had left us, "what do you make of it all?"

"I make nothing of it," I answered frankly. "It is a most mysterious business."

"As a rule," said Holmes, "the more bizarre a thing is the less mysterious it proves to be. It is your commonplace, featureless crimes which are really puzzling, just as a commonplace face is the most difficult to identify. But I must be prompt over this matter."

"What are you going to do, then?" I asked.

"To smoke," he answered. "It is quite a three pipe problem, and I beg that you won't speak to me for 50 minutes."

He curled himself up in his chair, with his thin knees drawn up to his hawk-like nose, and there he sat with his eyes closed and his black clay pipe thrusting out like the bill of some strange bird. I had come to the conclusion that he had dropped asleep, and indeed was nodding myself, when he suddenly sprang out of his chair with the gesture of a man who has made up his mind and put his pipe down upon the mantelpiece.

"Sarasate plays at the St. James's Hall this afternoon," he remarked. "What do you think, Watson? Could your patients spare you for a few hours?"

"I have nothing to do today. My practice is never very absorbing."

"Then put on your hat and come. I am going through the City first, and we can have some lunch on the way. I observe that there is a good deal of German music on the program, which is rather more to my taste than Italian or French. It is introspective, and I want to introspect. Come along!"

We traveled by the Underground as far as Aldersgate; and a short walk took us to Saxe-Coburg Square, the scene of the singular story which we had listened to in the morning. It was a poky, little, shabby-genteel place, where four lines of dingy two-storied brick houses looked out into a small railed-in enclosure, where a lawn of weedy grass and a few clumps of faded laurel-bushes made a hard fight against a smoke-laden and uncongenial atmosphere. Three gilt balls and a brown board with JABEZ WILSON in white letters, upon a corner house, announced the place where our red-headed client carried on his business.

Sherlock Holmes stopped in front of it with his head on one side and looked it all over, with his eyes shining brightly between puckered lids. Then he walked slowly up the street, and then down again to the corner, still looking keenly at the houses. Finally he returned to the pawnbroker's, and, having thumped vigorously upon the pavement with his stick two or three times, he went up to the door and knocked. It was instantly opened by a bright-looking, clean-shaven young fellow, who asked him to step in.

"Thank you," said Holmes, "I only wished to ask you how you would go from here to the Strand."

"Third right, fourth left," answered the assistant promptly, closing the door.

"Smart fellow, that," observed Holmes as we walked away. "He is, in my judgment, the fourth smartest man in London, and for daring I am not sure that he has not a claim to be third. I have known something of him before."

"Evidently," said I, "Mr. Wilson's assistant counts for a good deal in this mystery of the Red-headed League. I am sure that you inquired your way merely in order that you might see him."

"Not him."

"What then?"

"The knees of his trousers."

"And what did you see?"

"What I expected to see."

"Why did you beat the pavement?"

"My dear doctor, this is a time for observation, not for talk. We are spies in an enemy's country. We know something of Saxe-Coburg Square. Let us now explore the parts which lie behind it."

The road in which we found ourselves as we turned round the corner from the retired Saxe-Coburg Square presented as great a contrast to it as the front of a picture does to the back. It was one of the main arteries which conveyed the traffic of the City to the north and west. The roadway was blocked with the immense stream of commerce flowing in a double tide inward and outward, while the footpaths were black with the hurrying swarm of pedestrians. It was difficult to realize as we looked at the line of fine shops and stately business premises that they really abutted on the other side upon the faded and stagnant square which we had just quitted.

"Let me see," said Holmes, standing at the corner and glancing along the line, "I should like just to remember the order of the houses here. It is a hobby of mine to have an exact knowledge of London. There is Mortimer's, the tobacconist, the little newspaper shop, the Coburg branch of the City and Suburban Bank, the Vegetarian Restaurant, and McFarlane's carriage-building depot. That carries us right on to the other block. And now, Doctor, we've done our work, so it's time we had some play. A sandwich and a cup of coffee, and then off to violin-land, where all is sweetness and delicacy and harmony, and there are no red-headed clients to vex us with their conundrums."

My friend was an enthusiastic musician, being himself not only a very capable performer but a composer of no ordinary merit. All the afternoon he sat in the stalls wrapped in the most perfect happiness, gently waving his long, thin fingers in time to the music, while his gently smiling face and his languid, dreamy eyes were as unlike those of Holmes, the sleuth-hound, Holmes the relentless, keen-witted, ready-handed criminal agent, as it was possible to conceive. In his singular character the dual nature alternately asserted itself, and his extreme exactness and astuteness represented, as I have often thought, the reaction against the poetic and contemplative mood which occasionally predominated in him. The swing of his nature took him from extreme languor to devouring energy; and, as I knew well, he was never so truly formidable as when, for days on end, he had been lounging in his armchair amid his improvisations and his black-letter editions. Then it was that the lust of the chase would suddenly come upon him, and that his brilliant reasoning power would rise to the level of intuition, until those who were unacquainted with his methods would look askance at him as on a man whose knowledge was not that of other mortals. When I saw him that afternoon so enwrapped in the music at St. James's Hall I felt that an evil time might be coming upon those whom he had set himself to hunt down.

"You want to go home, no doubt, Doctor," he remarked as we emerged.

"Yes, it would be as well."

"And I have some business to do which will take some hours. This business at Coburg Square is serious."

"Why serious?"

"A considerable crime is in contemplation. I have every reason to believe that we shall be in time to stop it. But today being Saturday rather complicates matters. I shall want your help tonight."

"At what time?"

"Ten will be early enough."

"I shall be at Baker Street at 10."

"Very well. And, I say, Doctor, there may be some little danger, so kindly put your army revolver in your pocket." He waved his hand, turned on his heel, and disappeared in an instant among the crowd.

I trust that I am not more dense than my neighbors, but I was always oppressed with a sense of my own stupidity in my dealings with Sherlock Holmes. Here I had heard what he had heard, I had seen what he had seen, and yet from his words it was evident that he saw clearly not only what had happened but what was about to happen, while to me the whole business was still confused and grotesque. As I drove home to my house in Kensington I thought over it all, from the extraordinary story of the red-headed copier of the Encyclopedia down to the visit to Saxe-Coburg Square, and the ominous words with which he had parted from me. What was this nocturnal expedition, and why should I go armed? Where were we going, and what were we to do? I had the hint from Holmes that this smooth-faced pawnbroker's assistant was a formidable man—a man who might play a deep game. I tried to puzzle it out, but gave it up in despair and set the matter aside until night should bring an explanation.

It was a quarter-past nine when I started from home and

made my way across the Park, and so through Oxford Street to Baker Street. Two hansoms were standing at the door, and as I entered the passage I heard the sound of voices from above. On entering his room I found Holmes in animated conversation with two men, one of whom I recognized as Peter Jones, the official police agent, while the other was a long, thin, sad-faced man, with a very shiny hat and oppressively respectable frock-coat.

"Ha! Our party is complete," said Holmes, buttoning up his peajacket and taking his heavy hunting crop from the rack. "Watson, I think you know Mr. Jones, of Scotland Yard? Let me introduce you to Mr. Merryweather, who is to be our companion in tonight's adventure."

"We're hunting in couples again, Doctor, you see," said Jones in his consequential way. "Our friend here is a wonderful man for starting a chase. All he wants is an old dog to help him to do the running down."

"I hope a wild goose may not prove to be the end of our chase," observed Mr. Merryweather gloomily.

"You may place considerable confidence in Mr. Holmes, sir," said the police agent loftily. "He has his own little methods, which are, if he won't mind my saying so, just a little too theoretical and fantastic, but he has the makings of a detective in him. It is not too much to say that once or twice, as in that business of the Sholto murder and the Agra treasure, he has been more nearly correct than the official force."

"Oh, if you say so, Mr. Jones, it is all right," said the stranger with deference. "Still, I confess that I miss my card games. It is the first Saturday night in 27 years that I have not had my card game."

"I think you will find," said Sherlock Holmes, "that you will play for a higher stake tonight than you have ever done yet, and that the play will be more exciting. For you, Mr. Merryweather, the stake will be some 30,000 pounds; and for you, Jones, it will be the man upon whom you wish to lay your hands."

"John Clay, the murderer, thief, smasher, and forger. He's a young man, Mr. Merryweather, but he is at the head of his profession, and I would rather have my bracelets on him than on any criminal in London. He's a remarkable man, is young John Clay. His grandfather was a royal duke, and he himself has been to Eton and Oxford. His brain is as cunning as his fingers, and though we meet signs of him at every turn, we never know where to find the man himself. He'll crack a crib in Scotland one week, and be raising money to build an orphanage in Cornwall the next. I've been on his track for years and have never set eyes on him yet."

"I hope that I may have the pleasure of introducing you tonight. I've had one or two little turns also with Mr. John Clay, and I agree with you that he is at the head of his profession. It is past 10, however, and quite time that we started. If you two will take the first hansom, Watson and I will follow in the second."

Sherlock Holmes was not very communicative during the long drive and lay back in the cab humming the tunes which he had heard in the afternoon. We rattled through an endless labyrinth of gas-lit streets until we emerged into Farrington Street.

"We are close there now," my friend remarked. "This fellow Merryweather is a bank director, and personally interested in the matter. I thought it as well to have Jones with us also. He is not a bad fellow, though an absolute imbecile in his profession. He has one positive virtue. He is as brave as a bulldog and as tenacious as a lobster if he gets his claws upon anyone. Here we are, and they are waiting for us."

We had reached the same crowded thoroughfare in which we had found ourselves in the morning. Our cabs were dismissed, and, following the guidance of Mr. Merryweather, we passed down a narrow passage and through a side door, which he opened for us. Within there was a small corridor, which ended in a very massive iron gate. This also was opened, and led down a flight of winding stone steps, which terminated at another formidable gate. Mr. Merryweather stopped to light a lantern, and then conducted us down a dark, earth-smelling passage, and so, after opening a third door, into a huge vault or cellar, which was piled all round with crates and massive boxes.

"You are not very vulnerable from above," Holmes remarked as he held up the lantern and gazed about him.

"Nor from below," said Mr. Merryweather, striking his stick upon the flags which lined the floor. "Why, dear me, it sounds quite hollow!" he remarked, looking up in surprise.

"I must really ask you to be a little more quiet!" said Holmes severely. "You have already imperiled the whole success of our expedition. Might I beg that you would have the goodness to sit down upon one of those boxes, and not to interfere?"

The solemn Mr. Merryweather perched himself upon a crate, with a very injured expression upon his face, while Holmes fell upon his knees upon the floor and, with the lantern and a magnifying lens, began to examine minutely the cracks between the stones. A few seconds sufficed to satisfy him, for he sprang to his feet again and put his glass in his pocket.

"We have at least an hour before us," he remarked, "for they can hardly take any steps until the good pawnbroker is safely in bed. Then they will not lose a minute, for the sooner they do their work the longer time they will have for their escape. We are at present, Doctor—as no doubt you have divined—in the cellar of the City branch of one of the principal London banks. Mr. Merryweather is the chairman of directors, and he will explain to you that there are reasons why the more daring criminals of London should take a considerable interest in this cellar at present."

"It is our French gold," whispered the director. "We have had several warnings that an attempt might be made upon it."

"Your French gold?"

"Yes. We had occasion some months ago to strengthen our resources and borrowed for that purpose 30,000 napoleons from the Bank of France. It has become known that we have never had occasion to unpack the money, and that it is still lying in our cellar. The crate upon which I sit contains 2,000 napoleons packed between layers of lead foil. Our reserve of bullion is much larger at present than is usually kept in a single branch office, and the directors have had misgivings upon the subject."

"Which were very well justified," observed Holmes. "And now it is time that we arranged our little plans. I expect that within an hour matters will come to a head. In the meantime Mr. Merryweather, we must put the screen over that dark lantern."

"And sit in the dark?"

"I am afraid so. I had brought a pack of cards in my pocket, and I thought that, as we were a partie carree, you might have your game after all. But I see that the enemy's preparations have gone so far that we cannot risk the presence of a light. And, first of all, we must choose our positions. These are daring men, and though we shall take them at a disadvantage, they may do us some harm unless we are careful. I shall stand behind this crate, and do you conceal yourselves behind those. Then, when I flash a light upon them, close in swiftly. If they fire, Watson, have no compunction about shooting them down."

I placed my revolver, cocked, upon the top of the wooden case behind which I crouched. Holmes shot the slide across the front of his lantern and left us in pitch darkness —such an absolute darkness as I have never before experienced. The smell of hot metal remained to assure us that the light was still there, ready to flash out at a moment's notice. To me, with my nerves worked up to a pitch of expectancy, there was something depressing and subduing in the sudden gloom, and in the cold dank air of the vault.

"They have but one retreat," whispered Holmes. "That is back through the house into Saxe-Coburg Square. I hope that you have done what I asked you, Jones?"

"I have an inspector and two officers waiting at the front door."

"Then we have stopped all the holes. And now we must be silent and wait."

What a time it seemed! From comparing notes afterwards it was but an hour and a quarter, yet it appeared to me that the night must have almost gone, and the dawn be breaking above us. My limbs were weary and stiff, for I feared to change my position; yet my nerves were worked up to the highest pitch of tension, and my hearing was so acute that I could not only hear the gentle breathing of my companions, but I could distinguish the deeper, heavier in-breath of the bulky Jones from the thin, sighing note of the bank director. From my position I could look over the case in the direction of the floor. Suddenly my eyes caught the glint of a light.

At first it was but a lurid spark upon the stone pavement. Then it lengthened out until it became a yellow line, and then, without any warning or sound, a gash seemed to open and a hand appeared; a white, almost womanly hand, which felt about in the center of the little area of light. For a minute or more the hand, with its writhing fingers, protruded out of the floor. Then it was withdrawn as suddenly as it appeared, and all was dark again save the single lurid spark which marked a chink between the stones.

Its disappearance, however, was but momentary. With a rending, tearing sound, one of the broad, white stones turned over upon its side and left a square, gaping hole, through which streamed the light of a lantern. Over the edge there peeped a clean-cut, boyish face, which looked keenly about it, and then, with a hand on either side of the aperture, drew itself shoulder-high and waist-high, until one knee rested upon the edge. In another instant he stood at the side of the hole and was hauling after him a companion, lithe and small like himself, with a pale face and a shock of very red hair.

"It's all clear," he whispered. "Have you the chisel and the bags? Great Scott! Jump, Archie, jump, and I'll swing for it!"

Sherlock Holmes had sprung out and seized the intruder by the collar. The other dived down the hole, and I heard the sound of rending cloth as Jones clutched at his skirts. The light flashed upon the barrel of a revolver, but Holmes's hunting crop came down on the man's wrist, and the pistol clinked upon the stone floor.

"It's no use, John Clay," said Holmes blandly. "You have no chance at all."

"So I see," the other answered with the utmost coolness. "I fancy that my pal is all right, though I see you have got his coat-tails."

"There are three men waiting for him at the door," said Holmes.

"Oh, indeed! You seem to have done the thing very completely. I must compliment you."

"And I you," Holmes answered. "Your red-headed idea was very new and effective."

"You'll see your pal again presently," said Jones. "He's quicker at climbing down holes than I am. Just hold out while I fix the derbies."

"I beg that you will not touch me with your filthy hands," remarked our prisoner as the handcuffs clattered upon his wrists. "You may not be aware that I have royal blood in my veins. Have the goodness, also, when you address me always to say 'sir' and 'please.'"

"All right," said Jones with a stare and a snigger. "Well, would you please, sir, march upstairs, where we can get a cab to carry your Highness to the police-station?"

"That is better," said John Clay serenely. He made a sweeping bow to the three of us and walked quietly off in the custody of the detective.

"Really, Mr. Holmes," said Mr. Merryweather as we followed them from the cellar, "I do not know how the bank can thank you or repay you. There is no doubt that you have detected and defeated in the most complete manner one of the most determined attempts at bank robbery that have ever come within my experience."

"I have had one or two little scores of my own to settle with Mr. John Clay," said Holmes. "I have been at some small expense over this matter, which I shall expect the bank to refund, but beyond that I am amply repaid by having had an experience which is in many ways unique, and by hearing the very remarkable narrative of the Red-headed League."

"You see, Watson," he explained in the early hours of the morning as we sat over a glass of whisky and soda in Baker Street, "it was perfectly obvious from the first that the only possible object of this rather fantastic business of the advertisement of the League, and the copying of the Encyclopedia, must be to get this not over-bright pawnbroker out of the way for a number of hours every day. It was a curious way of managing it, but, really, it would be difficult to suggest a better. The method was no doubt suggested to Clay's ingenious mind by the color of his accomplice's hair. The four pounds a week was a lure which must draw him, and what was it to them, who were playing for thousands? They put in the advertisement, one rogue has the temporary office, the other rogue incites the man to apply for it, and together they manage to secure his absence every morning in the week. From the time that I heard of the assistant having come for half wages, it was obvious to me that he had some strong motive for securing the situation."

"But how could you guess what the motive was?"

"Had there been women in the house, I should have suspected a mere vulgar intrigue. That, however, was out of the question. The man's business was a small one, and there was nothing in his house which could account for such elaborate preparations, and such an expenditure as they were at. It must, then, be something out of the house. What could it be? I thought of the assistant's fondness for photography, and his trick of vanishing into the cellar. The cellar! There was the end of this tangled clue. Then I made inquiries as to this mysterious assistant and found that I had to deal with one of the coolest and most daring criminals in London. He was doing something in the cellar—something which took many hours a day for months on end. What could it be, once more? I could think of nothing save that he was running a tunnel to some other building.

"So far I had got when we went to visit the scene of action. I surprised you by beating upon the pavement with my stick. I was ascertaining whether the cellar stretched out in front or behind. It was not in front. Then I rang the bell, and, as I hoped, the assistant answered it. We have had some skirmishes, but we had never set eyes upon each other before. I hardly looked at his face. His knees were what I wished to see. You must yourself have remarked how worn, wrinkled, and stained they were. They spoke of those hours of burrowing. The only remaining point was what they were burrowing for. I walked round the corner, saw the City and Suburban Bank abutted on our friend's premises, and felt that I had solved my problem. When you drove home after the concert I called upon Scotland Yard and upon the chairman of the bank directors, with the result that you have seen."

"And how could you tell that they would make their attempt tonight?" I asked.

"Well, when they closed their League offices that was a sign that they cared no longer about Mr. Jabez Wilson's presence—in other words, that they had completed their tunnel. But it was essential that they should use it soon, as it might be discovered, or the bullion might be removed. Saturday would suit them better than any other day, as it would give them two days for their escape. For all these reasons I expected them to come tonight."

"You reasoned it out beautifully," I exclaimed in unfeigned admiration "It is so long a chain, and yet every link rings true."

"It saved me from ennui," he answered, yawning. "Alas! I already feel it closing in upon me. My life is spent in one long effort to escape from the commonplaces of existence. These little problems help me to do so."

"And you are a benefactor of the race," said I.

He shrugged his shoulders. "Well, perhaps, after all, it is of some little use," he remarked. "'L'homme c'est rien— l' oeuvre c'est tout,' as Gustave Flaubert wrote to George Sand."

THE ABSENCE OF MR. GLASS
FROM THE WISDOM OF FATHER BROWN

G. K. Chesterton

GILBERT KEITH CHESTERTON was born in London, England on May 29th, 1874. He began studying art, but soon found that his talent for argument was more suited to writing. Although he considered himself a mere "rollicking journalist," his literary talent extended to poetry, essays, novels, biographies, humorous tales, and mystery stories. Chesterton had very strong opinions and was extremely good at defending them. Fortunately, his outgoing and caring personality allowed him to maintain warm friendships with fellow authors such as George Bernard Shaw and H. G. Wells.

Chesterton disagreed bitterly with Sir Arthur Conan Doyle, author of another story in this collection. The two writers differed over the Boer War (1899–1902), in which British troops fought the descendents of Dutch settlers in South Africa. Chesterton publicly opposed the war, while Conan Doyle earned a knighthood for his service in the military and for his writings defending England's position.

Perhaps this explains why, in the following tale, Chesterton pokes fun at the famous detective, a character based on the great Sherlock Holmes. The hero

of the story turns out to be a simple country priest named Father Brown, Chesterton's most well known creation, who solves mysteries by his knowledge of human nature, rather than his reliance on evidence.

The consulting rooms of Dr. Orion Hood, the eminent criminologist and specialist in certain moral disorders, lay along the seafront at Scarborough, in a series of very large and well-lighted french windows, which showed the North Sea like one endless outer wall of blue-green marble. In such a place the sea had something of the monotony of a blue-green dado: for the chambers themselves were ruled throughout by a terrible tidiness not unlike the terrible tidiness of the sea. It must not be supposed that Dr. Hood's apartments excluded luxury, or even poetry. These things were there, in their place; but one felt that they were never allowed out of their place. Luxury was there: There stood upon a special table eight or ten boxes of the best cigars; but they were built upon a plan so that the strongest were always nearest the wall and the mildest nearest the window. A tantalus containing three kinds of spirit, all of a liqueur excellence, stood always on this table of luxury; but the fanciful have asserted that the whisky, brandy, and rum seemed always to stand at the same level. Poetry was there: The left-hand corner of the room was lined with as complete a set of English classics as the right hand could show of English and foreign physiologists. But if one took a volume of Chaucer or Shelley from that rank, its absence irritated the mind like a gap in a man's front teeth. One could not say the books were never read; probably they were, but there was a sense of their being chained to their places, like the bibles in the old churches. Dr. Hood treated his private bookshelf as if it were a public library. And if this strict scientific intangibility steeped even the shelves laden with lyrics and ballads and the tables laden with drink and tobacco, it goes without saying that yet more of such heathen holiness protected the other shelves that held the specialist's library, and the other tables that sustained the frail and even fairylike instruments of chemistry or mechanics.

Dr. Hood paced the length of his string of apartments, bounded—as the boys' geographies say—on the east by the North Sea and on the west by the serried ranks of his sociological and criminologist library. He was clad in an artist's velvet, but with none of an artist's negligence; his hair was heavily shot with gray, but growing thick and healthy; his face was lean, but sanguine and expectant. Everything about him and his room indicated something at once rigid and restless, like that great northern sea by which (on pure principles of hygiene) he had built his home.

Fate, being in a funny mood, pushed the door open and introduced into those long, strict, sea-flanked apartments one who was perhaps the most startling opposite of them and their master. In answer to a curt but civil summons, the door opened inward and there shambled into the room a shapeless little figure, which seemed to find its own hat and umbrella as unmanageable as a mass of luggage. The umbrella was a black and prosaic bundle long past repair; the hat was a broad-curved black hat, clerical but not common in England; the man was the very embodiment of all that is homely and helpless.

The doctor regarded the newcomer with a restrained astonishment, not unlike that he would have shown if some huge but obviously harmless seabeast had crawled into his room. The newcomer regarded the doctor with that beaming but breathless geniality which characterizes a corpulent charwoman who has just managed to stuff herself into an omnibus. It is a rich confusion of social self-congratulation and bodily disarray. His hat tumbled to the carpet, his heavy umbrella slipped between his knees with a thud; he reached after the one and ducked after the other, but with an unimpaired smile on his round face spoke simultaneously as follows:

"My name is Brown. Pray excuse me. I've come about that business of the MacNabs. I have heard, you often help people out of such troubles. Pray excuse me if I am wrong."

By this time he had sprawlingly recovered the hat, and made an odd little bobbing bow over it, as if setting everything quite right.

"I hardly understand you," replied the scientist, with a cold intensity of manner. "I fear you have mistaken the chambers. I am Dr. Hood, and my work is almost entirely literary and educational. It is true that I have sometimes been consulted by the police in cases of peculiar difficulty and importance, but—"

"Oh, this is of the greatest importance," broke in the little man called Brown. "Why, her mother won't let them get engaged." And he leaned back in his chair in radiant rationality.

The brows of Dr. Hood were drawn down darkly, but the eyes under them were bright with something that might be anger or might be amusement. "And still," he said, "I do not quite understand."

"You see, they want to get married," said the man with the clerical hat. "Maggie MacNab and young Todhunter want to get married. Now, what can be more important than that?"

The great Orion Hood's scientific triumphs had deprived him of many things—some said of his health, others of his God; but they had not wholly despoiled him of his sense of the absurd. At the last plea of the ingenuous priest a chuckle broke out of him from inside, and he threw himself into an armchair in an ironical attitude of the consulting physician.

"Mr. Brown," he said gravely, "it is quite 14½ years since I was personally asked to test a personal problem: then it was the case of an attempt to poison the French president at a Lord Mayor's banquet. It is now, I understand, a question of whether some friend of yours called Maggie is a suitable fiancée for some friend of hers called Todhunter. Well, Mr. Brown, I am a sportsman. I will take it on. I will give the MacNab family my best advice, as good as I gave the French Republic and the king of England—no, better: 14 years better. I have nothing else to do this afternoon. Tell me your story."

The little clergyman called Brown thanked him with unquestionable warmth, but still with a queer kind of simplicity. It was rather as if he were thanking a stranger in a smoking room for some trouble in passing the matches, than as if he were (as he was) practically thanking the curator of Kew Gardens for coming with him into a field to find a four-leaved clover. With scarcely a semicolon after his hearty thanks, the little man began his recital:

"I told you my name was Brown; well, that's the fact, and I'm the priest of the little Catholic church I dare say you've seen beyond those straggly streets, where the town ends toward the north. In the last and straggliest of those streets which runs along the sea like a seawall there is a very honest but rather sharp-tempered member of my flock, a widow called MacNab. She has one daughter, and she lets lodgings, and between her and the daughter, and between her and the lodgers—well, I dare say there is a great deal to be said on both sides. At present she has only one lodger, the young man called Todhunter; but he has given more trouble than all the rest, for he wants to marry the young woman of the house."

"And the young woman of the house," asked Dr. Hood, with huge and silent amusement, "what does she want?"

"Why, she wants to marry him," cried Father Brown, sitting up eagerly. "That is just the awful complication."

"It is indeed a hideous enigma," said Dr. Hood.

"This young James Todhunter," continued the cleric, "is a very decent man so far as I know; but then nobody knows very much. He is a bright, brownish little fellow, agile like a monkey, clean-shaven like an actor, and obliging like a born courtier. He seems to have quite a pocketful of money, but nobody knows what his trade is. Mrs. MacNab, therefore (being of a pessimistic turn), is quite sure it is something dreadful, and probably connected with dynamite. The dynamite must be of a shy and noiseless sort, for the poor fellow only shuts himself up for several hours of the day and studies something behind a locked door. He declares his privacy is temporary and justified, and promises to explain before the wedding. That is all that anyone knows for certain, but Mrs. MacNab will tell you a great deal more than even she is certain of. You know how the tales grow like grass on such a patch of ignorance as that. There are tales of two voices heard talking in the room; though, when the door is opened, Todhunter is always found alone. There are tales of a mysterious tall man in a silk hat, who once came out of the seamists and apparently out of the sea, stepping softly across the sandy fields and through the small back garden at twilight, till he was heard talking to the lodger at his open window. The colloquy seemed to end in a quarrel. Todhunter dashed down his window with violence, and the man in the high hat melted into the seafog again. This story is told by the family with the fiercest mystification; but I really think Mrs. Mac-Nab prefers her own original tale: that the other man (or whatever it is) crawls out every night from the big box in the corner, which is kept locked all day. You see, therefore, how this sealed door of Todhunter's is treated as the gate of all the fancies and monstrosities of the 'Thousand and One Nights.' And yet there is the little fellow in his respectable black jacket, as punctual and innocent as a parlor clock. He pays his rent to the tick; he is practically a teetotaler; he is tirelessly kind with the younger children, and can keep them amused for a day on end; and, last and most urgent of all, he has made himself equally popular with the eldest daughter, who is ready to go to church with him tomorrow."

A man warmly concerned with any large theories has always a relish for applying them to any triviality. The great specialist having condescended to the priest's simplicity, condescended expansively. He settled himself with comfort in his armchair and began to talk in the tone of a somewhat ab-sentminded lecturer:

"Even in a minute instance, it is best to look first to the main tendencies of Nature. A particular flower may not be dead in early winter, but the flowers are dying; a particular pebble may never be wetted with the tide, but the tide is coming in. To the scientific eye all human history is a series of collective movements, destructions or migrations, like the massacre of flies in winter or the return of birds in spring. Now the root fact in all history is Race. Race produces reli-gion; Race produces legal and ethical wars. There is no stronger case than that of the wild, unworldly and perishing stock which we commonly call the Celts, of whom your friends the MacNabs are specimens. Small, swarthy, and of this dreamy and drifting blood, they accept easily the su-perstitious explanation of any incidents, just as they still ac-cept (you will excuse me for saying) that superstitious explanation of all incidents which you and your Church rep-resent. It is not remarkable that such people, with the sea moaning behind them and the Church (excuse me again) droning in front of them, should put fantastic features into what are probably plain events. You, with your small parochial responsibilities, see only this particular Mrs. Mac-Nab, terrified with this particular tale of two voices and a tall man out of the sea. But the man with the scientific imag-ination sees, as it were, the whole clans of MacNab scat-tered over the whole world, in its ultimate average as uniform as a tribe of birds. He sees thousands of Mrs. Mac-Nabs, in thousands of houses, dropping their little drop of morbidity in the tea-cups of their friends; he sees—"

Before the scientist could conclude his sentence, another and more impatient summons sounded from without; someone with swishing skirts was marshaled hurriedly down the corridor, and the door opened on a young girl, decently dressed but disordered and red-hot with haste. She had sea-blown blond hair, and would have been entirely beautiful if her cheekbones had not been, in the Scotch manner, a little high in relief as well as in color. Her apology was almost as abrupt as a command.

"I'm sorry to interrupt you, sir," she said, "but I had to follow Father Brown at once; it's nothing less than life or death."

Father Brown began to get to his feet in some disorder. "Why, what has happened, Maggie?" he said.

"James has been murdered, for all I can make out," answered the girl, still breathing hard from her rush. "That man Glass has been with him again; I heard them talking through the door quite plain. Two separate voices: for James speaks low, with a burr, and the other voice was high and quavery."

"That man Glass?" repeated the priest in a tone of some perplexity.

"I know his name is Glass," answered the girl, in great impatience. "I heard it through the door. They were quarreling—about money, I think—for I heard James say again and again, 'That's right, Mr. Glass,' or 'No, Mr. Glass,' and then, 'Two or three, Mr. Glass.' But we're talking too much; you must come at once, and there may be time yet."

"But time for what?" asked Dr. Hood, who had been studying the young lady with marked interest. "What is there about Mr. Glass and his money troubles that should impel such urgency?"

"I tried to break down the door and couldn't," answered the girl shortly, "Then I ran to the backyard, and managed to climb onto the windowsill that looks into the room. It was dim, and seemed to be empty, but I swear I saw James lying huddled up in a corner, as if he were drugged or strangled."

"This is very serious," said Father Brown, gathering his errant hat and umbrella and standing up; "in point of fact I was just putting your case before this gentleman, and his view—"

"Has been largely altered," said the scientist gravely. "I do not think this young lady is so Celtic as I had supposed. As I have nothing else to do, I will put on my hat and stroll down town with you."

In a few minutes all three were approaching the dreary tail of the MacNabs's street: the girl with the stern and breathless stride of the mountaineer, the criminologist with a lounging grace (which was not without a certain leopardlike swiftness), and the priest at an energetic trot entirely devoid of distinction. The aspect of this edge of the town was not entirely without justification for the doctor's hints about desolate moods and environments. The scattered houses stood farther and farther apart in a broken string along the seashore; the afternoon was closing with a premature and partly lurid twilight; the sea was of an inky purple and murmuring ominously. In the scrappy back garden of the MacNabs which ran down toward the sand, two black, barren-looking trees stood up like demon hands held up in astonishment, and as Mrs. MacNab ran down the street to meet them with lean hands similarly spread, and her fierce face in shadow, she was a little like a demon herself. The doctor and the priest made scant reply to her shrill reiterations of her daughter's story, with more disturbing details of her own, to the divided vows of vengeance against Mr. Glass for murdering, and against Mr. Todhunter for being murdered, or against the latter for having dared to want to marry her daughter, and for not having lived to do it. They passed through the narrow passage in the front of the house until they came to the lodger's door at the back, and there Dr. Hood, with the trick of an old detective, put his shoulder sharply to the panel and burst in the door.

It opened on a scene of silent catastrophe. No one seeing it, even for a flash, could doubt that the room had been the theater of some thrilling collision between two, or perhaps more, persons. Playing cards lay littered across the table or fluttered about the floor as if a game had been interrupted. Two wine glasses stood ready for wine on a side table, but a third lay smashed in a star of crystal upon the carpet. A few feet from it lay what looked like a long knife or short sword, straight, but with an ornamental and pictured handle, its dull blade just caught a gray glint from the dreary window behind, which showed the black trees against the leaden level of the sea. Toward the opposite corner of the room was rolled a gentleman's silk top hat, as if it had just been knocked off his head; so much so, indeed, that one almost looked to see it still rolling. And in the corner behind it, thrown like a sack of potatoes, but corded like a railway trunk, lay Mr. James Todhunter, with a scarf across his mouth, and six or seven ropes knotted round his elbows and ankles. His brown eyes were alive and shifted alertly.

Dr. Orion Hood paused for one instant on the doormat and drank in the whole scene of voiceless violence. Then he stepped swiftly across the carpet, picked up the tall silk hat, and gravely put it upon the head of the yet pinioned Tod-hunter. It was so much too large for him that it almost slipped down onto his shoulders.

"Mr. Glass's hat," said the doctor, returning with it and peering into the inside with a pocket lens. "How to explain the absence of Mr. Glass and the presence of Mr. Glass's hat? For Mr. Glass is not a careless man with his clothes. That hat is of a stylish shape and systematically brushed and burnished, though not very new. An old dandy, I should think."

"But, good heavens!" called out Miss MacNab, "aren't you going to untie the man first?"

"I say 'old' with intention, though not with certainty" continued the expositor; "my reason for it might seem a little far-fetched. The hair of human beings falls out in very varying degrees, but almost always falls out slightly, and with the lens I should see the tiny hairs in a hat recently worn. It has none, which leads me to guess that Mr. Glass is bald. Now when this is taken with the high-pitched and querulous voice which Miss MacNab described so vividly (patience, my dear lady, patience), when we take the hairless head together with the tone common in senile anger, I should think we may deduce some advance in years. Nevertheless, he was probably vigorous, and he was almost certainly tall. I might rely in some degree on the story of his previous appearance at the window, as a tall man in a silk hat, but I think I have more exact indication. This wineglass has been smashed all over the place, but one of its splinters lies on the high bracket beside the mantelpiece. No such fragment could have fallen there if the vessel had been smashed in the hand of a comparatively short man like Mr. Todhunter."

"By the way," said Father Brown, "might it not be as well to untie Mr. Todhunter?"

"Our lesson from the drinking-vessels does not end here," proceeded the specialist. "I may say at once that it is possible that the man Glass was bald or nervous through dissipation rather than age. Mr. Todhunter, as has been remarked, is a quiet thrifty gentleman, essentially an abstainer. These cards and wine cups are no part of his normal habit; they have been produced for a particular companion. But, as it happens, we may go farther. Mr. Todhunter may or may not possess this wine service, but there is no appearance of his possessing any wine. What, then, were these vessels to contain? I would at once suggest some brandy or whisky, perhaps of a luxurious sort, from a flask in the pocket of Mr. Glass. We have thus something like a picture of the man, or at least of the type: tall, elderly, fashionable, but somewhat frayed, certainly fond of play and strong waters, perhaps rather too fond of them. Mr. Glass is a gentleman not unknown on the fringes of society."

"Look here," cried the young woman, "if you don't let me pass to untie him I'll run outside and scream for the police."

"I should not advise you, Miss MacNab," said Dr. Hood gravely, "to be in any hurry to fetch the police. Father Brown, I seriously ask you to compose your flock, for their sakes, not for mine. Well, we have seen something of the figure and quality of Mr. Glass; what are the chief facts known of Mr. Todhunter? They are substantially three: that he is

economical, that he is more or less wealthy, and that he has a secret. Now, surely it is obvious that there are the three chief marks of the kind of man who is blackmailed. And surely it is equally obvious that the faded finery, the profligate habits, and the shrill irritation of Mr. Glass are the unmistakable marks of the kind of man who blackmails him. We have the two typical figures of a tragedy of hush money: on the one hand, the respectable man with a mystery; on the other, the West End vulture with a scent for a mystery. These two men have met here today and have quarreled, using blows and a bare weapon."

"Are you going to take those ropes off?" asked the girl stubbornly.

Dr. Hood replaced the silk hat carefully on the side table, and went across to the captive. He studied him intently, even moving him a little and half turning him round by the shoulders, but he only answered:

"No; I think these ropes will do very well till your friends the police bring the handcuffs."

Father Brown, who had been looking dully at the carpet, lifted his round face and said: "What do you mean?"

The man of science had picked up the peculiar dagger sword from the carpet and was examining it intently as he answered:

"Because you find Mr. Todhunter tied up," he said, "you all jump to the conclusion that Mr. Glass had tied him up; and then, I suppose, escaped. There are four objections to this: First, why should a gentleman so dressy as our friend Glass leave his hat behind him, if he left of his own free will? Second," he continued, moving toward the window,

69

"this is the only exit, and it is locked on the inside. Third, this blade here has a tiny touch of blood at the point, but there is no wound on Mr. Todhunter. Mr. Glass took that wound away with him, dead or alive. Add to all this primary probability. It is much more likely that the blackmailed person would try to kill his incubus, rather than that the blackmailer would try to kill the goose that lays his golden egg. There, I think, we have a pretty complete story."

"But the ropes?" inquired the priest, whose eyes had remained open with a rather vacant admiration.

"Ah, the ropes," said the expert with a singular intonation. "Miss MacNab very much wanted to know why I did not set Mr. Todhunter free from his ropes. Well, I will tell her. I did not do it because Mr. Todhunter can set himself free from them at any minute he chooses."

"What?" cried the audience on quite different notes of astonishment.

"I have looked at all the knots on Mr. Todhunter," reiterated Hood quietly. "I happen to know something about knots; they are quite a branch of criminal science. Every one of those knots he has made himself and could loosen himself; not one of them would have been made by an enemy really trying to pinion him. The whole of this affair of the ropes is a clever fake, to make us think him the victim of the struggle instead of the wretched Glass, whose corpse may be hidden in the garden or stuffed up the chimney."

There was a rather depressed silence; the room was darkening, the sea-blighted boughs of the garden trees looked leaner and blacker than ever, yet they seemed to have come nearer to the window. One could almost fancy they were sea-monsters like krakens or cuttlefish, writhing polyps who had crawled up from the sea to see the end of this tragedy, even as he, the villain and victim of it, the terrible man in the tall hat, had once crawled up from the sea. For the whole air was dense with the morbidity of blackmail, which is the most morbid of human things because it is a crime concealing a crime; a black plaster on a blacker wound.

The face of the little Catholic priest, which was commonly complacent and even comic, had suddenly become knotted with a curious frown. It was not the blank curiosity of his first innocence. It was rather that creative curiosity which comes when a man has the beginnings of an idea. "Say it again, please," he said in a simple, bothered manner; "do you mean that Todhunter can tie himself up all alone and untie himself all alone?"

"That is what I mean," said the doctor.

"Jerusalem!" shouted Brown suddenly, "I wonder if it could possibly be that!"

He scuttled across the room rather like a rabbit, and peered with quite a new impulsiveness into the partially covered face of the captive. Then he turned his own rather fatuous face to the company. "Yes, that's it!" he cried in a certain excitement. "Can't you see it in the man's face? Why, look at his eyes!"

Both the professor and the girl followed the direction of his glance. And though the broad black scarf completely masked the lower half of Todhunter's visage, they did grow conscious of something struggling and intense about the upper part of it.

71

"His eyes do look queer," cried the young woman, strongly moved. "You brutes; I believe it's hurting him!"

"Not that, I think," said Dr. Hood; "the eyes have certainly a singular expression. But I should interpret those transverse wrinkles as expressing rather such slight psychological abnormality—"

"Oh, bosh!" cried Father Brown: "can't you see he's laughing?"

"Laughing!" repeated the doctor, with a start; "but what on earth can he be laughing at?"

"Well," replied the Reverend Brown apologetically, "not to put too fine a point on it, I think he is laughing at you. And indeed, I'm a little inclined to laugh at myself, now I know about it."

"Now you know about what?" asked Hood, in some exasperation.

"Now I know," replied the priest, "the profession of Mr. Todhunter."

He shuffled about the room, looking at one object after another with what seemed to be a vacant stare, and then invariably bursting into an equally vacant laugh, a highly irritating process for those who had to watch it. He laughed very much over the hat, still more uproariously over the broken glass, but the blood on the sword point sent him into mortal convulsions of amusement. Then he turned to the fuming specialist.

"Dr. Hood," he cried enthusiastically, "you are a great poet! You have called an uncreated being out of the void. How much more godlike that is than if you had only ferreted out the mere facts! Indeed, the mere facts are rather commonplace and comic by comparison."

"I have no notion what you are talking about," said Dr. Hood rather haughtily; "my facts are all inevitable, though necessarily incomplete. A place may be permitted to intuition, perhaps (or poetry if you prefer the term), but only because the corresponding details cannot as yet be ascertained. In the absence of Mr. Glass—"

"That's it, that's it," said the little priest, nodding quite eagerly, "that's the first idea to get fixed; the absence of Mr. Glass. He is so extremely absent. I suppose," he added reflectively, "that there was never anybody so absent as Mr. Glass."

"Do you mean he is absent from the town?" demanded the doctor.

"I mean he is absent from everywhere," answered Father Brown; "he is absent from the nature of things, so to speak."

"Do you seriously mean," said the specialist with a smile, "that there is no such person?"

The priest made a sign of assent. "It does seem a pity," he said.

Orion Hood broke into a contemptuous laugh. "Well," he said, "before we go on to the hundred and one other evidences, let us take the first proof we found; the first fact we fell over when we fell into this room. If there is no Mr. Glass, whose hat is this?"

"It is Mr. Todhunter's," replied Father Brown.

"But it doesn't fit him," cried Hood impatiently. "He couldn't possibly wear it!"

Father Brown shook his head with ineffable mildness. "I never said he could wear it," he answered. "I said it was his hat. Or, if you insist on a shade of difference, a hat that is his."

"And what is the shade of difference?" asked the criminologist with a slight sneer.

"My good sir," cried the mild little man, with his first movement akin to impatience, "if you will walk down the street to the nearest hatter's shop, you will see that there is, in common speech, a difference between a man's hat and the hats that are his."

"But a hatter," protested Hood, "can get money out of his stock of new hats. What could Todhunter get out of this one old hat?"

"Rabbits," replied Father Brown promptly.

"What?" cried Dr. Hood.

"Rabbits, ribbons, sweetmeats, goldfish, rolls of colored paper," said the reverend gentleman with rapidity. "Didn't you see it all when you found out the faked ropes? It's just the same with the sword. Mr. Todhunter hasn't got a scratch on him, as you say; but he's got a scratch in him, if you follow me."

"Do you mean inside Mr. Todhunter's clothes?" inquired Mrs. MacNab sternly.

"I do not mean inside Mr. Todhunter's clothes," said Father Brown. "I mean inside Mr. Todhunter."

"Well, what in the name of Bedlam do you mean?"

"Mr. Todhunter," explained Father Brown placidly, "is learning to be a professional conjurer, as well as juggler, ventriloquist, and expert in the rope trick. The conjuring explains the hat. It is without traces of hair, not because it is worn by the prematurely bald Mr. Glass, but because it has never been worn by anybody. The juggling explains the three glasses, which Todhunter was teaching himself to throw up and catch in rotation. But, being only at the stage of practice, he smashed one glass against the ceiling. And the juggling also explains the sword, which it was Mr. Todhunter's professional pride and duty to swallow. But, again, being at the stage of practice, he very slightly grazed the inside of his throat with the weapon. Hence he has a wound inside him, which I am sure (from the expression on his face) is not a serious one. He was also practicing the trick of a release from ropes, like the Davenport brothers, and he was just about to free himself when we all burst into the room. The cards, of course, are for card tricks, and they are scattered on the floor because he had just been practicing one of those dodges of sending them flying through the air. He merely kept his trade secret, because he had to keep his tricks secret, like any other conjurer. But the mere fact of an idler in a top hat having once looked in at his back window, and been driven away by him with great indignation, was enough to set us all on a wrong track of romance, and make us imagine his whole life overshadowed by the silk-hatted specter of Mr. Glass."

"But what about the two voices?" asked Maggie, staring.

"Have you never heard a ventriloquist?" asked Father Brown. "Don't you know they speak first in their natural voice, and then answer themselves in just that shrill, squeaky, unnatural voice that you heard?"

There was a long silence, and Dr. Hood regarded the little man who had spoken with a dark and attentive smile. "You are certainly a very ingenious person," he said; "it could not have been done better in a book. But there is just one part of Mr. Glass you have not succeeded in explaining away, and that is his name. Miss MacNab distinctly heard him so addressed by Mr. Todhunter."

The Rev. Mr. Brown broke into a rather childish giggle. "Well, that," he said, "that's the silliest part of the whole silly story. When our juggling friend here threw up the three glasses in turn, he counted them aloud as he caught them, and also commented aloud when he failed to catch them. What he really said was: 'One, two and three—missed a glass one, two—missed a glass.' And so on."

There was a second of stillness in the room, and then everyone with one accord burst out laughing. As they did so the figure in the corner complacently uncoiled all the ropes and let them fall with a flourish. Then, advancing into the middle of the room with a bow, he produced from his pocket a big bill printed in blue and red, which announced that Zaladin, the world's greatest conjurer, contortionist, ventriloquist and human kangaroo would be ready with an entirely new series of tricks at the Empire Pavilion, Scarborough, on Monday next at eight o'clock precisely.

GOOD LADY DUCAYNE

Mary Elizabeth Braddon
(1835–1915)

MARY ELIZABETH BRADDON was born in London on October 4, 1835. When she was only four, Braddon's parents separated, leaving the mother and daughter to find a way to support themselves. Unfortunately, there were not many careers open to women in those days and Braddon did not have the benefit of a formal education. She decided to become an actress to earn enough money to support herself and her mother, however the life of a stage actress was considered improper for a lady. In 1860, after the completion of *The Loves of Arcadia*, Braddon ended her acting career and began writing full-time. During her long career she penned more than 80 novels and nine more plays. She even created a new category of fiction, the "sensation novel," which became the most popular style of novel in the 1860s. Her most famous book, *Lady Audley's Secret*, was an overnight success when it appeared in 1862 and quickly became one of the best-selling novels of the nineteenth century.

Although she had left the stage, Braddon remained a controversial figure. She and her publisher, John Maxwell, lived together for many years and had six children, even though he was married to another woman living in an insane asylum. Braddon and Maxwell eventually did marry on October 2, 1874, a month after Maxwell's wife died.

"Good Lady Ducayne" is a fascinating tale of mystery and horror involving an affluent old lady and her fanatical desire to prolong her life. Although two companions have already died in this woman's service, the unsuspecting Bella Rolleston agrees to take the vacant position. It is not long before she begins to suffer from gruesome "mosquito bites" and terrible dreams. Can it be these disturbing symptoms are threatening her life?

I

Bella Rolleston had made up her mind that her only chance of earning her bread and helping her mother to an occasional crust was by going out into the great unknown world as a companion to a lady. She was willing to go to any lady rich enough to pay her a salary and so eccentric as to wish for a hired companion. Five solid shillings had been handed to a smartly-dressed lady in an office in Harbeck Street, London, W., in the hope that this very Superior Person would find a situation and a salary for Miss Rolleston. The Superior Person glanced at the two half-crowns as they lay on the table where Bella's hand had placed them, to make sure they were neither of them florins, before she wrote a description of Bella's qualifications and requirements in a formidable-looking ledger.

"Age?" she asked, curtly.

"Eighteen, last July."

"Any accomplishments?"

"No; I am not at all accomplished. If I were I should want to be a governess—a companion seems the lowest stage."

"We have some highly accomplished ladies on our books as companions, or chaperon companions."

"Oh, I know!" babbled Bella, loquacious in her youthful candor. "But that is quite a different thing. Mother hasn't been able to afford a piano since I was twelve years old, so I'm afraid I've forgotten how to play. And I have had to help mother with her needlework, so there hasn't been much time to study."

"Please don't waste time upon explaining what you can't do, but kindly tell me anything you can do," said the Superior Person, crushingly, with her pen poised between delicate fingers waiting to write. "Can you read aloud for two or three hours at a stretch? Are you active and handy, an early riser, a good walker, sweet tempered, and obliging?"

"I can say yes to all those questions except about the sweetness. I think I have a pretty good temper, and I should be anxious to oblige anybody who paid for my services. I should want them to feel that I was really earning my salary."

"The kind of ladies who come to me would not care for a talkative companion. My connection lies chiefly among the aristocracy, and in that class considerable deference is expected."

"Oh, of course," said Bella; "but it's quite different when I'm talking to you. I want to tell you all about myself."

"I am glad it is to be only once!" said the Person, with the edges of her lips.

"Do you think you have anything on your books that would suit me?" faltered Bella, after a pause.

"Oh, dear, no; I have nothing in view at present," answered the Person, who had swept Bella's half-crowns into a drawer, absentmindedly, with the tips of her fingers. "You see, you are so very unformed—so much too young to be companion to a lady of position. It is a pity you have not enough education for a nursery governess; that would be more in your line."

"And do you think it will be very long before you can get me a situation?" asked Bella, doubtfully.

"I really cannot say. Have you any particular reason for being so impatient—not a love affair, I hope?"

"A love affair!" cried Bella, with red cheeks. "I want a situation because my mother is poor, and I hate being a burden to her."

"There won't be much margin for sharing in the salary you are likely to get at your age," said the Person, who found Bella's bright eyes and unbridled vivacity oppressive.

"Perhaps if you'd be kind enough to give me back the fee I could take it to an agency where the connection isn't quite so aristocratic," said Bella, who—as she told her mother in her recital of the interview—was determined not to be sat upon.

"You will find no agency that can do more for you than mine," replied the Person, whose harpy fingers never relinquished a coin. "You will have to wait for your opportunity. Yours is an exceptional case: but I will bear you in mind, and if anything suitable offers I will write to you."

The half-contemptuous bend of the stately head, weighted with borrowed hair, indicated the end of the interview.

II

Mrs. Rolleston was a lady by birth and education; but it had been her bad fortune to marry a scoundrel; for the last half-dozen years she had been that worst of widows, a wife whose husband had deserted her. Happily, she was courageous, industrious, and a clever needlewoman; and she had been able just to earn a living for herself and her only child, by making mantles and cloaks for a West-end house. It was not a luxurious living. Cheap lodgings in a shabby street off the Walworth Road, scanty dinners, homely food, well-worn raiment, had been the portion of mother and daughter; but they loved each other so dearly, and Nature had made them both so light-hearted, that they had contrived somehow to be happy.

But now this idea of going out into the world as companion to some fine lady had rooted itself into Bella's mind, and although she idolized her mother, and although the parting of mother and daughter must needs tear two loving hearts into shreds, the girl longed for enterprise and change and excitement, as the pages of old longed to be knights.

She grew tired of racing downstairs every time the postman knocked, only to be told, "nothing for you, miss," till at last Bella walked up to Harbeck Street, and asked the Superior Person how it was that no situation had been found for her.

"You are too young," said the Person, "and want a salary."

"Of course I do," answered Bella; "don't other people?"

"Young ladies your age generally want a comfortable home."

"I don't," snapped Bella: "I want to help my mother."

"If I hear of anything," said the Person, "I will write you."

No letter came from the Person, and in exactly a week Bella put on her neatest hat, and trudged off to Harbeck Street.

The Person's office was at the further end, and Bella looked down that long, gray vista almost despairingly, more tired than usual with the trudge from Walworth. As she looked, a carriage passed her, an old-fashioned, yellow chariot, on cee springs, drawn by a pair of high gray horses, with the stateliest of coachmen driving them, and a tall footman sitting by his side.

"It looks like the fairy godmother's coach," thought Bella. "I shouldn't wonder if it began by being a pumpkin."

It was a surprise when she reached the Person's door to find the yellow chariot standing before it. She was almost afraid to go in and meet the owner of that splendid carriage. She had caught only a glimpse of its occupant as the chariot rolled by, a plumed bonnet, a patch of ermine.

The Person's smart page ushered her upstairs and knocked at the official door. "Miss Rolleston," he announced.

"Show her in," said the Person, quickly; and then Bella heard her murmuring something in a low voice to her client.

Bella went in fresh, blooming, a living image of youth and hope, and before she looked at the Person her gaze was riveted by the owner of the chariot.

Never had she seen anyone as old as the old lady sitting by the Person's fire: a little old figure, wrapped from chin to feet in an ermine mantle; a withered, old face under a plumed bonnet—a face so wasted by age that it seemed only a pair of eyes and a peaked chin. The nose was peaked, too, but between the sharply pointed chin and the great, shining eyes, the small, aquiline nose was hardly visible.

"This is Miss Rolleston, Lady Ducayne."

Claw-like fingers, flashing with jewels, lifted a double eye-glass to Lady Ducayne's shining black eyes, and through the glasses Bella saw those unnaturally bright eyes magnified to a gigantic size, and glaring at her awfully.

"Miss Torpinter has told me all about you," said the old voice that belonged to the eyes. "Have you got good health? Are you strong and active, able to eat well, sleep well, walk well, able to enjoy all that there is good in life?"

"I have never known what it is to be ill, or idle."

"Then I think you will do for me."

"Of course, in the event of references being satisfactory," put in the Person.

"I don't want references. The young woman looks frank and innocent. I'll take her on trust. I want a strong young woman whose health will give me no trouble."

"You have been so unfortunate in that respect," cooed the Person, whose voice and manner were subdued to a melting sweetness by the old woman's presence. "But I am sure Miss Rolleston will not disappoint you, though certainly after your unpleasant experience with Miss Tomson, who looked the picture of health— and Miss Blandy, who said she had never seen a doctor since she was vaccinated"

"Lies, no doubt," muttered Lady Ducayne, then turning to Bella, she asked, curtly, "You don't mind spending the winter in Italy, I suppose?"

"It has been the dream of my life to see Italy," she gasped.

"Well, your dream will be realized. Get yourself ready to leave Charing Cross by the train deluxe this day week at eleven. Be sure you are at the station a quarter before the hour. My people will look after you and your luggage."

Lady Ducayne rose from her chair, assisted by her crutch-stick, and Miss Torpinter escorted her to the door.

"And with regard to salary?" asked the Person on the way.

"Salary, oh, the same as usual—and if the young woman wants a quarter's pay in advance you can write to me for a check," Lady Ducayne answered, carelessly.

Miss Torpinter went all the way downstairs with her client, and waited to see her seated in the yellow chariot. When she came upstairs again she was slightly out of breath, and she had resumed that superior manner which Bella had found so crushing.

"You may think yourself lucky, Miss Rolleston," she said. "I have dozens of young ladies on my books whom I might have recommended for this situation—but I remembered having told you to call this afternoon—and I thought I would give you a chance. Old Lady Ducayne is one of the best people on my books. She gives her companion a hundred a year, and pays all traveling expenses. You will live in the lap of luxury."

"A hundred a year! How too lovely! Shall I have to dress very grandly? Does Lady Ducayne keep much company?"

"At her age! No, she lives in seclusion—in her own apartments—her French maid, her footman, her medical attendant, her courier."

"Why did those other companions leave her?" asked Bella.

"Their health broke down!"

"Poor things, and so they had to leave!"

"Yes, they had to leave. I suppose you would like a quarter's salary in advance?"

"Oh, yes, please. I shall have things to buy."

"Very well, I will write for Lady Ducayne's check, and I will send you the balance—after deducting my commission."

III

From Miss Rolleston, at Cap Ferrino,
to Mrs. Rolleston, in Beresford Street,
Walworth, London.

How I wish you could see this place, dearest; the blue sky, the olive woods, the orange and lemon orchards between the cliffs and the sea—sheltering in the hollow of the great hills—and with summer waves dancing up to the narrow ridge of pebbles and weeds which is the Italian idea of a beach! Oh, how I wish you could see it all, mother dear, and bask in this sunshine, that makes it so difficult to believe the date at the head of this paper. November! The air is like an English June—the sun is so hot that I can't walk a few yards without an umbrella.

You could never imagine the luxury of this hotel. It is nearly new, and has been built and decorated regardless of expense. Our rooms are upholstered in pale blue satin, which shows up Lady Ducayne's parchment complexion; but as she sits all day long in a corner of the balcony basking in the sun, except when she is in her carriage, and all the evening in her arm-chair close to the fire, and never sees anyone but her own people, her complexion matters very little.

She has the handsomest suite of rooms in the hotel. My bedroom is inside hers, the sweetest room—all blue satin and white lace—white enameled furniture, looking-glasses on every wall, till I know my pert little profile as I never knew it before.

I feel as if Lady Ducayne were a funny old grandmother, who had suddenly appeared in my life, very, very rich, and very, very kind. She is not at all exacting. I read aloud to her a good deal, and she dozes and nods while I read. Sometimes I hear her moaning in her sleep—as if she has troublesome dreams. When she is tired of my reading she orders Francine, her maid, to read a French novel to her. My French is not good enough to follow Francine, who reads very quickly.

I have a great deal of liberty, for Lady Ducayne often tells me to run away and amuse myself; I roam about the hills for hours. Everything is so lovely. Sometimes I go no farther than the terrace in front of the hotel, which is a favorite lounging-place. The gardens lie below, and the tennis courts where I sometimes play with a very nice girl. She is a year older than I, and has come to Cap Ferrino with her brother, a medical student. He came to Italy entirely on his sister's account. She had a troublesome chest attack last summer and was ordered to winter abroad. They are orphans, quite alone in the world, and so fond of each other. It is very nice for me to have such a friend as Lotta. She is so thoroughly respectable. I can't help using that word, for some of the girls in this hotel go on in a way that I know you would shudder at. Lotta was brought up by an aunt, deep down in the country, and knows hardly anything about life. Her brother won't allow her to read a novel, French or English, that he has not read and approved.

Perhaps this is what makes some girls so eager to marry—the want of someone strong and brave and honest and true to care for them and order them about. I want no one, mother darling, for I have you, and you are all the world to me. No husband could ever come between us two. If I ever were to marry he would have only the second place in my heart. But I don't suppose I ever shall marry, or even know what it is like to have an offer of marriage. No young man can afford to marry a penniless girl nowadays. Life is too expensive.

Mr. Stafford, Lotta's brother, is very clever, and very kind. He thinks it is rather hard for me to have to live with such an old woman as Lady Ducayne, but then he does not know how poor we are and what a wonderful life this seems to me in this lovely place. I feel a selfish wretch for enjoying all my luxuries, while you, who want them so much more than I, have none of them.

This letter was written when Bella had been less than a month at Cap Ferrino, before the novelty had worn off the landscape, and before the pleasure of luxurious surroundings had begun to cloy. She wrote to her mother every week, such long letters as girls who have lived in closest companionship with a mother alone can write; letters that are like a diary of heart and mind. She wrote gaily always; but when the new year began Mrs. Rolleston thought she detected a note of melancholy under all those lively details about the place and the people.

"My poor girl is getting homesick," she thought.

It might be that she missed her new friend and companion, Lotta Stafford, who had gone with her brother for a little tour to Genoa and Spezia, and as far as Pisa. They were to return before February; but in the meantime Bella might naturally feel very solitary among all those strangers, whose manners and doings she described so well.

The mother's instinct had been true. Bella was not so happy as she had been in that first flush of wonder and delight. Somehow, she knew not how, lassitude had crept upon her. She thought of Beresford Street and her mother's face with a sick longing. They were so far—so far away! And then she thought of Lady Ducayne, sitting by the heaped-up olive logs in the overheated salon—thought of that wizened-nutcracker profile, and those gleaming eyes, with an invincible horror.

Visitors at the hotel had told her that the air of Cap Ferrino was relaxing—better suited to age than youth, to sickness than to health. No doubt it was so. She was not so well as she had been at Walworth; but she told herself that she was suffering only from the pain of separation from the dear companion of her girlhood, the mother who had been nurse, sister, friend, flatterer, all things in this world to her.

She was sitting in her favorite spot, an angle at the eastern end of the terrace, a quiet little nook sheltered by orange trees, when she heard a couple of Riviera habitués talking in the garden below. They were sitting on a bench against the terrace wall.

She had no idea of listening to their talk, till the sound of Lady Ducayne's name attracted her, and then she listened without any thought of wrong-doing. They were talking no secrets—just casually discussing a hotel acquaintance.

They were two elderly people whom Bella only knew by sight. An English clergyman who had wintered abroad for half his lifetime; a stout, comfortable, well-to-do spinster, whose chronic bronchitis obliged her to migrate annually.

"I have met her about Italy for the last ten years," said the lady, "but have never found out her real age."

"I put her down at a hundred—not a year less," replied the parson. "Her reminiscences all go back to the Regency. She was evidently then in her zenith, and I have heard her say things that showed she was in Parisian society when the First Empire was at its best—before Josephine was divorced."

"She doesn't talk much now."

"No; there's not much life left in her. She is wise in keeping herself secluded. I only wonder that wicked old quack, her Italian doctor, didn't finish her off years ago."

"I should think that he keeps her alive."

"My dear Miss Manders, do you think foreign quackery ever kept anybody alive?"

"Well, there she is—and she never goes anywhere without him. He certainly has an unpleasant countenance."

"Unpleasant," echoed the parson, "The foul fiend himself can beat him in ugliness. I pity that poor young woman who has to live between old Lady Ducayne and Dr. Parravicini."

"But the old lady is very good to her companions."

"No doubt. She is very free with her cash; the servants call her good Lady Ducayne. I daresay she's generous to those poor girls—but she can't make them happy. They die in her service."

"Don't say they, Mr. Carton; I know that one poor girl died at Mentone last spring."

"Yes, and another poor girl died in Rome three years ago. I was there at the time. Good Lady Ducayne left her there in an English family. The girl had every comfort. The old woman was very liberal to her—but she died. I tell you, Miss Manders, it is not good for any young woman to live with two such horrors as Lady Ducayne and Parravicini."

They talked of other things—but Bella hardly heard them. She sat motionless, and a cold wind seemed to come down upon her from the mountains and to creep up to her from the sea, till she shivered as she sat there in the sunshine.

Yes, they were uncanny, certainly, the pair of them— she so like an aristocratic witch in her withered old age; he of no particular age, with a face that was more like a waxen mask than any human countenance Bella had ever seen. What did it matter? Old age is venerable, and worthy of all reverence; and Lady Ducayne had been very kind to her. Dr. Parravicini was a harmless, inoffensive student, who seldom looked up from the book he was reading. He had his private sitting-room, where he made experiments in chemistry and natural science—perhaps in alchemy. What could it matter to Bella? He had always been polite to her, in his far-off way. She could not be more happily placed than she was—in his palatial hotel, with this rich old lady.

No doubt she missed the young English girl who had been so friendly, and it might be that she missed the girl's brother, for Mr. Stafford had talked to her a good deal—had interested himself in the books she was reading, and her manner of amusing herself when she was not on duty.

Sometimes she found herself wondering whether she would ever see her beloved mother again. Strange forebodings came into her mind. She was angry with herself for giving way to melancholy thoughts.

One day she questioned Lady Ducayne's French maid about those two companions who had died within three years.

"They were poor, feeble creatures," Francine told her. "They looked fresh and bright enough when they came to Milady; but they ate too much, and they were lazy. They died of luxury and idleness. Milady was too kind to them. They had nothing to do; and so they took to fancying things; fancying the air didn't suit them, that they couldn't sleep."

"I sleep well enough, but I have had a strange dream several times since I have been in Italy."

"Ah, you had better not begin to think about dreams, or you will be like those other girls. They were dreamers—and they dreamt themselves into the cemetery."

The dream troubled her a little, not because it was a ghastly or frightening dream, but on account of sensations which she had never felt before in sleep—a whirring of wheels that went round in her brain, a great noise like a whirlwind, but rhythmi-cal like the ticking of a gigantic clock: and then in the midst of this uproar as of winds and waves she seemed to sink into a gulf of unconsciousness, out of sleep into far deeper sleep—total extinction. And then, after that black interval, there had come the sound of voices, and then again the whirr of wheels, louder and louder—and again the black—and then she awoke, feeling languid and oppressed.

She told Dr. Parravicini of her dream one day, on the only occasion when she wanted his professional advice. She had suffered severely from the mosquitoes before Christmas—and had been almost frightened at finding a wound upon her arm which she could only attribute to the venomous sting of one of these torturers. Parravicini put on his glasses, and scrutinized the angry mark on the round, white arm, as Bella stood before him and Lady Ducayne with her sleeve rolled up above her elbow.

"He has caught you on the top of a vein," he said. "What a vampire! But there's no harm done, signorina, nothing that a little dressing of mine won't heal. You must always show me any bite of this nature. It might be dangerous if neglected."

"And to think that such tiny creatures can bite like this," said Bella; "my arm looks as if it had been cut by a knife."

"If I were to show you a mosquito's sting under my microscope you wouldn't be surprised at that," replied Parravicini.

Bella had to put up with the mosquito bites, even when they came on the top of a vein, and produced that ugly wound. The wound recurred now and then at longish intervals, and Bella found Dr. Parravicini's dressing a speedy cure. If he were the quack his enemies called him, he had at least a light hand and a delicate touch in performing this small operation.

Bella Rolleston to Mrs. Rolleston
April 14th.

Ever Dearest,

Behold the check for my second quarter's salary—
5 and 20 pounds. There is no one to pinch off a year's commission as there was last time, so it is all for you, mother, dear.

You ask me so earnestly if I am quite well that I fear my letters must have been very dull lately. Yes, dear, I am well—but I am not quite so strong as I was when I used to trudge to the West-end to buy half a pound of tea. Italy is relaxing; and I feel what the people here call 'slack.' But I fancy I can see your dear face looking worried as you read this. Indeed, I am not ill. I am only a little tired of this lovely scene.

My friend Lotta and her brother never came back after all. They went from Pisa to Rome. Happy mortals! And they are to be on the Italian lakes in May; which lake was not decided when Lotta last wrote to me. She has been a charming correspondent, and has confided all her little flirtations to me. We are all to go to Bellaggio next week—by Genoa and Milan. Isn't that lovely?

Love and love—and ever more love from your adoring,

BELLA.

IV

Herbert Stafford and his sister had often talked of the pretty English girl with her fresh complexion, which made such a pleasant touch of rosy color among all those sallow faces at the Grand Hotel. The young doctor thought of Bella with a tenderness—her utter loneliness in that great hotel where there were so many people, her bondage to that old, old woman, where everybody else was free to think of nothing but enjoying life. It was a hard fate; and the poor child was evidently devoted to her mother, and felt the pain of separation.

Lotta told him one morning that they were to meet again at Bellagio. "The old thing and her court are to be there before we are," she said. "I shall be charmed to have Bella again. She is so bright and gay—in spite of an occasional touch of homesickness."

"I like her best when she is homesick," said Herbert; "for then I am sure she has a heart."

"What have you to do with hearts, except for dissection? Don't forget that Bella is an absolute pauper. She told me in confidence that her mother makes mantles for a West-end shop. You couldn't marry a girl whose mother makes mantles."

"We haven't come to the consideration of that question yet," answered Herbert, who liked to provoke his sister.

In two years' hospital practice he had seen too much of the grim realities of life to retain any prejudices about rank.

Mr. Stafford and his sister arrived at Bellaggio in a fair May evening. The sun was going down as the steamer approached the pier; and all that glory of purple bloom which curtains every wall at this season of the year flushed and deepened in the glowing light. A group of ladies were standing on the pier watching the arrivals, and among them Herbert saw a pale face that startled him out of his wonted composure.

"There she is," murmured Lotta, at his elbow, "but how dreadfully changed. She looks a wreck."

They were shaking hands with her a few minutes later, and a flush had lighted up her poor pinched face in the pleasure of meeting.

"I thought you might come this evening," she said. "We have been here a week."

"Oh, you poor darling, how awfully ill you must have been," exclaimed Lotta, as the two girls embraced.

"No, no, I have not been ill—I have only felt a little weaker than I used to be. I don't think the air of Cap Ferrino quite agreed with me."

"It must have disagreed with you abominably. I never saw such a change in anyone. Do let Herbert doctor you. He is fully qualified, you know."

"I am sure he must be very clever!" faltered Bella, "but there is really nothing the matter. I am not ill, and if I were ill, Lady Ducayne's physician—"

"That dreadful man with the yellow face? I hope you haven't been taking any of his medicines."

"No, dear, I have taken nothing. I have never complained of being ill."

This was said while they were all three walking to the hotel. The Staffords' rooms had been secured in advance, pretty ground-floor rooms, opening into the garden. Lady Ducayne's statelier apartments were on the floor above.

"I believe these rooms are just under ours," said Bella.

"Then it will be all the easier for you to run down to us," replied Lotta, which was not really the case, as the grand staircase was in the center of the hotel.

"Oh, I shall find it easy enough," said Bella. "I'm afraid you'll have too much of my society. Lady Ducayne sleeps away half the day in this warm weather, so I have a good deal of idle time; and I get awfully moped thinking of mother and home."

Her voice broke upon the last words. She was homesick and she had dreams; or, rather, an occasional recurrence of that one bad dream with all its strange sensations—it was more like a hallucination than dreaming—the whirring of wheels, the sinking into an abyss, the struggling back to consciousness. She had the dream shortly before she left Cap Ferrino, but not since she had come to Bellaggio, and she began to hope the air in this lake district suited her better, and that those strange sensations would never return.

Mr. Stafford wrote a prescription and had it made up at the chemist's near the hotel. It was a powerful tonic, and after two bottles, and a row or two on the lake, and some rambling over the hills and in the meadows where the spring flowers made earth seem paradise, Bella's spirits and looks improved as if by magic.

"It is a wonderful tonic," she said, but perhaps in her heart of hearts she knew that the doctor's kind voice, and the friendly hand that helped her in and out of the boat, and the lake, had something to do with her cure.

"I hope you don't forget that her mother makes mantles," Lotta said warningly.

"I fear your poor friend may not live to be any man's wife."

"Do you think her so very ill?"

He sighed, and left the question unanswered.

One day, while they were gathering wild hyacinths in an upland meadow, Bella told Mr. Stafford about her bad dream.

"It is curious only because it is hardly like a dream," she said. "I daresay you could find some commonsense reason for it. The position of my head on my pillow, or the atmosphere."

And then she described her sensations; how in the midst of sleep there came a sudden sense of suffocation; and then those whirring wheels, so loud, so terrible; and then a blank, and then a coming back to waking consciousness.

"Have you ever had chloroform given you—by a dentist?"

"Never—Dr. Parravicini asked me that question one day."

"Lately?"

"No, long ago, when we were in the train deluxe."

"Has Dr. Parravicini prescribed for you since you began to feel weak and ill?"

"Oh, he has given me a tonic from time to time, but I took very little. I am not ill, only weaker than I used to be. I was ridiculously strong and well when I lived at Walworth."

"You don't look strong now, you poor dear," said Lotta.

"I'm afraid Italy doesn't agree with me."

"Perhaps it is not Italy, but being cooped up with Lady Ducayne that has made you ill."

"But I am never cooped up. Lady Ducayne is absurdly kind, and lets me roam about or sit in the balcony all day if I like. I have read more novels since I have been with her than in all the rest of my life."

"Then she is very different from the average old lady, who is usually a slave driver," said Stafford. "I wonder why she carries a companion with her if she has so little need of society."

"Oh, I am only part of her state. She is inordinately rich—and the salary she gives me doesn't count. Apropos of Dr. Parravicini, I know he is a clever doctor, for he cures my horrid mosquito bites."

"A little ammonia would do that, in the early stage of the mischief. But there are no mosquitoes to trouble you now."

"Oh, yes, there are; I had a bite just before we left Cap Ferrino." She pushed up her loose lawn sleeve, and exhibited a scar, which he scrutinized intently, with a surprised look.

"This is no mosquito bite," he said.

"Oh, yes it is—unless there are snakes at Cap Ferrino."

"It is not a bite at all. You are trifling with me. Miss Rolleston—you have allowed that wretched Italian quack to bleed you. They killed the greatest man in modern Europe that way, remember. How very foolish of you."

"I was never bled in my life, Mr. Stafford."

"Nonsense! Let me look at your other arm. Are there any more mosquito bites?"

"Yes; Dr. Parravicini says I have a bad skin for healing, and that the poison acts more virulently with me than with most."

Stafford examined both her arms in the broad sunlight, scars new and old.

"You have been very badly bitten, Miss Rolleston," he said, "and if ever I find the mosquito I shall make him smart. But, now tell me, my dear girl, on your word of honor, tell me as you would tell a friend who is sincerely anxious for your health and happiness—as you would tell your mother if she were here to question you—have you no knowledge of any cause for these scars except mosquito bites—no suspicion even?"

"No, indeed! No, upon my honor! I have never seen a mosquito biting my arm. One never does see the horrid little fiends. But I have heard them trumpeting under the curtains and I know that I have often had one of the pestilent wretches buzzing about me."

Later Bella and her friends were sitting at tea in the garden, while Lady Ducayne took her afternoon drive with her doctor.

"How long do you mean to stop with Lady Ducayne, Miss Rolleston?" Herbert Stafford asked, after a thoughtful silence.

"As long as she will go on paying me."

"Even if you feel your health breaking down in her service?"

"It is not the service that has injured my health. You can see that I have really nothing to do—to read aloud for an hour or so once or twice a week; to write a letter once in a while to a London tradesman. I shall never have such an easy time with anybody. And nobody else would give me a hundred a year."

"Then you mean to go on till you die at your post?"

"Like the other two companions? No! If ever I feel seriously ill—really ill—I shall put myself in a train and go back to Walworth without stopping."

"What about the other two companions?"

"They both died. It was very unlucky for Lady Ducayne. That's why she engaged me; she chose me because I was ruddy and robust. She must feel rather disgusted at my having grown white and weak. By-the-bye, when I told her about the good your tonic had done me, she said she would like to see you and have a little talk with you about her own case."

"Will you ask her if she will see me this evening?"

"With pleasure! I wonder what you will think of her? She looks rather terrible to a stranger; but Dr. Parravicini says she was once a famous beauty."

It was nearly 10 o'clock when Mr. Stafford was summoned by message from Lady Ducayne, whose courier came to conduct him to her ladyship's salon. Bella was reading aloud when the visitor was admitted; and he noticed the languor in the low, sweet tones, the evident effort.

"Shut up the book," said the querulous old voice. "You are beginning to drawl like Miss Blandy."

Stafford saw a small, bent figure crouching over the piled

up olive logs; a shrunken old figure in a gorgeous garment of black and crimson brocade, a skinny throat emerging from a mass of old Venetian lace, clasped with diamonds that flashed like fireflies as the trembling old head turned toward him.

The eyes that looked at him were almost as bright as the diamonds—the only living feature in that narrow parchment mask. He had seen terrible faces in the hospital—faces on which disease had set dreadful marks—but he had never seen a face that impressed him so painfully as this withered countenance, with its indescribable horror of death outlived, a face that should have been hidden under a coffin-lid years ago.

The Italian physician was standing on the other side of the fireplace, smoking a cigarette, and looking down at the little old woman over the hearth as if he were proud of her.

"Good evening, Mr. Stafford; you can go to your room, Bella, and write your everlasting letter to your mother at Walworth," said Lady Ducayne. "I believe she writes a page about every wild flower she discovers in the woods and meadows. I don't know what else she can find to write about," she added, as Bella quietly withdrew to the pretty little bedroom opening out of Lady Ducayne's spacious apartment. Here, as at Cap Ferrino, she slept in a room adjoining the old lady's.

"You are a medical man, I understand, Mr. Stafford."

"I am qualified, but I have not begun to practice."

"You have begun upon my companion, she tells me."

"I have prescribed for her, and I am happy my prescription has done her good; but I look upon that improvement as temporary. Her case will require more drastic treatment."

"Never mind her case. There is nothing the matter with the girl—absolutely nothing—except girlish nonsense; too much liberty and not enough work."

"I understand that two of your previous companions died of the same disease," said Stafford, looking first at Lady Ducayne, and then at Parravicini, whose yellow complexion had paled a little under Stafford's scrutiny.

"Don't bother me about my companions, sir," said Lady Ducayne. "I sent for you to consult you about myself—not about a parcel of anemic girls. You are young, and medicine is a progressive science. Where have you studied?"

"In Edinburgh—and in Paris."

"Good schools. You have studied hypnotism—electricity?"

"And the transfusion of blood," said Stafford, very slowly, looking at Parravicini.

"Have you made any discovery that teaches you to pro-long human life—any elixir—any mode of treatment? I want my life prolonged, young man. That man there has been my physician for thirty years. He does all he can to keep me alive. He studies all the new theories of all the scientists—but he is old; he gets older every day—his brain-power is going—he is bigoted—prejudiced —can't receive new ideas—can't grapple with new systems. He will let me die if I am not on my guard against him. Come, Mr. Stafford, I am a rich woman. Give me a few years more in the sunshine, a few years more above ground, and I will give you the price of a fashionable London practice—I will set you up at the West-end."

"How old are you, Lady Ducayne?"

"I was born the day Louis XVI was guillotined."

"Then I think you have had your share of the sunshine and the pleasures of the earth, and that you should spend your few remaining days in repenting your sins and trying to make atonement for the young lives that have been sacrificed to your love of life."

"What do you mean by that, sir?"

"Oh, Lady Ducayne, need I put your wickedness and your physician's still greater wickedness in plain words? The poor girl who is now in your employment has been reduced from robust health to a condition of absolute danger by Dr. Parravicini's experimental surgery; and I have no doubt those other two young women who broke down in your service were treated by him in the same manner. I could take upon myself to demonstrate—by most convincing evidence, to a jury of medical men—that Dr. Parravicini has been bleeding Miss Rolleston after putting her under chloroform, at intervals, ever since she has been in your service. The deterioration in the girl's health speaks for itself; the lancet marks upon the girl's arms are unmistakable; and her description of a series of sensations, which she calls a dream, points unmistakably to the administration of chloroform while she was sleeping. A practice so nefarious, so murderous, must, if exposed, result in a sentence only less severe than the punishment of murder."

"I laugh," said Parravicini, with an airy motion of his skinny fingers; "I laugh at once at your theories and at your threats. I, Leopold Parravicini, have no fear that the law can question anything I have done."

"Take the girl away, and let me hear no more of her," cried Lady Ducayne, in the thin, old voice, which so poorly matched the energy and fire of the wicked old brain that

guided its utterances. "Let her go back to her mother—
I want no more girls to die in my service. There are girls
enough and to spare in the world, God knows."

"If you ever engage another companion—or take another
English girl into your service, Lady Ducayne, I will make all
England ring with the story of your wickedness."

"I want no more girls. I don't believe in his experiments.
They have been full of danger for me as well as for the girl—
an air bubble, and I should be gone. I'll have no more of his
dangerous quackery. I'll find some new man—a better man
than you, sir, a discoverer like Pasteur, or Virchow, a genius—to keep me alive. Take your girl away, young man.
Marry her if you like. I'll write a check for a thousand
pounds, and let her go and live on beef and beer, and get
strong and plump again. I'll have no more such experiments.
Do you hear, Parravicini?" she screamed, vindictively.

The Staffords carried Bella Rolleston off to Varese the
next day, she very loath to leave Lady Ducayne, whose liberal salary afforded such help for her dear mother. Herbert
Stafford insisted, however, treating Bella as coolly as if he
had been the family physician, and she had been given over
wholly to his care.

"Do you suppose your mother would let you stop here to
die?" he asked. "If Mrs. Rolleston knew how ill you are, she
would come post haste to fetch you."

"I shall never be well again till I get back to Walworth,"
answered Bella, who was low-spirited and inclined to tears.

"We'll try a week or two at Varese first," said Stafford.
"When you can walk halfway up Monte Generoso without
palpitation of the heart, you shall go back to Walworth."

"Poor mother, how glad she will be to see me, and how sorry that I've lost such a good place."

This conversation took place on the boat when they were leaving Bellaggio. Lotta had gone to her friend's room at seven o'clock that morning, long before Lady Ducayne's withered eyelids had opened to the daylight, before even Francine, the French maid, was astir, and had helped pack a bag with essentials, and hustled Bella downstairs and out of doors before she could make any strenuous resistance.

"It's all right," Lotta assured her. "Herbert had a good talk with Lady Ducayne last night, and it was settled for you to leave this morning. She doesn't like invalids, you see."

"No," sighed Bella, "she doesn't like invalids. It was unlucky that I should break down, like Miss Tomson and Miss Blandy."

"At any rate, you are not dead, like them," answered Lotta, "and my brother says you are not going to die."

It seemed rather a dreadful thing to be dismissed in that offhand way, without a word of farewell from her employer.

"I wonder what Miss Torpinter will say when I go to her for another situation," Bella speculated, ruefully, while she and her friends were breakfasting on board the steamer.

"You may never want another situation," said Stafford.

"You mean that I may never be well enough to be useful?"

"No, I don't mean anything of the kind."

It was after dinner at Varese, when Bella had been induced to take a whole glass of Chianti, and quite sparkled after that unaccustomed stimulant, that Mr. Stafford produced a letter from his pocket. "I forgot to give you Lady Ducayne's letter of adieu!" he said.

"What, did she write to me? I am so glad—I hated to leave her in such a cool way; for after all she was very kind to me, and if I didn't like her it was only because she was too dreadfully old."

She tore open the envelope. The letter was to the point:

Goodbye, child. Go and marry your doctor.
I enclose a farewell gift for your trousseau.

ADELINE DUCAYNE

"A hundred pounds, a whole year's salary—no—why, it's for a—a check for a thousand!" cried Bella. "What a generous old soul! She really is the dearest old thing."

"She just missed being dear to you, Bella," said Stafford.

He had dropped into the use of her Christian name while they were on board the boat. It seemed natural now that she was to be in his charge till they all three went back to England.

"I shall take upon myself the privileges of an elder brother till we land at Dover," he said; "after that —well, it must be as you please."

The question of their future relations must have been satisfactorily settled before they crossed the Channel, for Bella's next letter to her mother communicated three startling facts.

First, that the enclosed check for £1,000 was to be invested in debenture stock in Mrs. Rolleston's name, and was to be her very own, income and principal, for the rest of her life.

Next, that Bella was going home to Walworth immediately.

And last, that she was going to be married to Mr. Herbert Stafford in the following autumn.

"And I am sure you will adore him, mother, as much as I do," wrote Bella. "It is all good Lady Ducayne's doing. I never could have married if I had not secured that little nest-egg for you. Herbert says we shall be able to add to it as the years go by, and that wherever we live there shall be always a room for you. The word 'mother-in-law' has no terrors for him."

THE
STORY OF THE GOBLINS
WHO STOLE A SEXTON
FROM PICKWICK PAPERS,
(1836)

Charles Dickens
(1812–1870)

CHARLES DICKENS was born near Portsmouth, England in February of 1812. For several years the family lived quite happily, but eventually Dickens' father moved them all to London. This turned out to be an unlucky move, for Mr. Dickens, who was never very good with money matters, was suddenly arrested for debt. In those days, if people could not pay their bills, they were sent to debtors' prison! Twelve-year-old Charles was forced to quit school and went to work in a shoe-dyeing factory. He lived alone, ashamed, and frightened. Although his father later inherited some money, this experience made Charles very sympathetic to orphans and the poor, about whom he often wrote.

Charles Dickens created many unforgettable characters, including Fagin from *Oliver Twist* and Wackford Squeers, the wicked schoolmaster from *Nicholas Nickleby*. Dickens was always searching for names for these creations, and he carried around a small notebook where he wrote down any unusual names he came across. He thought the name should match the character's personality. One of his most famous characters, with a name to match, is Ebenezer Scrooge from *A Christmas Carol*. Those who have seen *A Christmas Carol* as a play or a movie, or who have read the original story will find the tale below somewhat familiar. The spirits you are about to meet, however, are a far more vicious bunch than the three Mr. Scrooge encounters.

In an old abbey town, down in this part of the country, a long, long, while ago—so long, that the story must be a true one, because our great-grandfathers believed it— there officiated as sexton and grave-digger in the churchyard, one Gabriel Grub. Gabriel Grub was an ill-conditioned, cross-grained, surly fellow—a morose and lonely man, who consorted with nobody but himself, and an old wicker bottle which fitted into his large deep waistcoat pocket—and who eyed each merry face as it passed him by with such a deep scowl of malice and ill-humor, as it was difficult to meet without feeling something the worse for.

A little before twilight one Christmas Eve Gabriel shouldered his spade, lighted his lantern, and betook himself towards the old churchyard; for he had a grave to finish by next morning, and, feeling very low, he thought it might raise his spirits, perhaps, if he went on with his work at once. As he went his way, up the ancient street, he saw the cheerful light of the blazing fires gleam through the old casements, and heard the loud laugh and the cheerful shouts of those who

were assembled around them. He marked the bustling preparations for next day's cheer, and smelt the numerous savory
odors consequent thereupon, as they steamed up from the
kitchen windows in clouds. All this was gall and wormwood
to the heart of Gabriel Grub, and when groups of children
bounded out of the houses, tripped across the road, and were
met, before they could knock at the opposite door, by half a
dozen curly-headed little rascals who crowded round them as
they flocked upstairs to spend the evening in their Christmas
games, Gabriel smiled grimly and clutched the handle of his
spade with a firmer grasp as he thought of the measles, scar-
let-fever, thrush, and whooping-cough they might contract.

In this happy frame of mind, Gabriel strode along, returning a short, sullen growl to the good-humored greetings of his
neighbors as now and then passed him until he turned into the
dark lane which led to the churchyard. Now, Gabriel had been
looking forward to reaching the dark lane, because it was, generally speaking, a nice, gloomy, mournful place into which
the townspeople did not much care to go, except in broad daylight, and when the sun was shining; consequently, he was in-
dignant to hear a young urchin roaring out some jolly song
about a merry Christmas, in this very sanctuary, which had
been called Coffin Lane ever since the days of the old abbey,
and the time of the shaven-headed monks. As Gabriel walked
on, and the voice drew nearer, he found it came from a small
boy who was hurrying along to join one of the little parties in
the old street, and who, partly to keep himself company, and
partly to prepare himself for the occasion, was shouting out the
song at the highest pitch of his lungs. So Gabriel waited until
the boy came up, and then pushed him into a corner and

rapped him over the head with his lantern five or six times, to teach him to control his voice. And as the boy hurried away with his hand to his head, singing quite a different sort of tune, Gabriel Grub chuckled very heartily to himself and entered the churchyard, locking the gate behind him.

He took off his coat, put down his lantern, and getting into the unfinished grave, worked at it for an hour or so. But the earth was hardened with the frost, and it was not easy to break it up and shovel it out. Although there was a moon, it was a very young one and shed little light upon the grave, which was in the shadow of the church. At any other time, these obstacles would have made Gabriel Grub very moody and miserable, but he was so well pleased with having stopped the small boy's singing that he took little heed of the scanty progress he had made, and looked down into the grave when he had finished work for the night, with grim satisfaction: murmuring as he gathered up his things:

> Brave lodgings for one, brave lodgings for one,
> A few feet of cold earth, when life is done;
> A stone at the head, a stone at the feet,
> A rich, juicy meal for the worms to eat;
> Rank grass over head, and damp clay around,
> Brave lodgings for one, these, in holy ground!

"Ho! Ho!" laughed Gabriel Grub, as he sat himself down on a flat tombstone which was a favorite resting place of his and drew forth his wicker bottle. "A coffin at Christmas! A Christmas box. Ho! ho! ho!"

"Ho! ho! ho!" repeated a voice which sounded close behind the sexton.

Gabriel paused in some alarm, in the act of raising the wicker bottle to his lips, and looked round. The bottom of the oldest grave about him was as still and quiet as the churchyard in the pale moonlight. The cold frost glistened on the tombstones, and sparkled like rows of gems among the stone carvings of the old church. The snow lay hard and crisp upon the ground and spread over the thickly-strewn mounds of earth so white and smooth a cover that it seemed as if corpses lay there, hidden only by their winding sheets. Not the faintest rustle broke the profound tranquility of the solemn scene. Sound itself appeared to be frozen up, all was so cold and still.

"It was the echoes," said Gabriel Grub, raising the bottle to his lips again.

"It was *not*," said a deep voice.

Gabriel started up and stood rooted to the spot with astonishment and terror. His eyes rested on a form that made his blood run cold.

Seated on an upright tombstone close to him was a strange unearthly figure, whom Gabriel felt at once was no being of this world. His long fantastic legs, which might have reached the ground, were cocked up, and crossed after a quaint, fantastic fashion; his sinewy arms were bare, and his hands rested on his knees. On his short round body he wore a close covering, ornamented with small slashes; a short cloak dangled at his back, the collar cut into curious peaks, which served the goblin in place of a neckerchief; and his shoes curled at his toes into long points. On his head, he wore a broad-brimmed sugar-loaf hat, garnished with a single feather. The hat was covered with the white frost, and the goblin looked as if he had sat on the same tombstone very comfortably for two or three hundred years. He was sitting perfectly still; his tongue was out, as if in derision, and he was grinning at Gabriel Grub with such a grin as only a goblin could call up.

"It was *not* the echoes," said the goblin.

Gabriel Grub was paralyzed, and could make no reply.

"What do you do here on Christmas Eve?" said the goblin sternly.

"I came to dig a grave, sir," stammered Gabriel Grub.

"What man wanders among graves and churchyards on such a night as this?" cried the goblin.

"Gabriel Grub! Gabriel Grub!" screamed a wild chorus of voices that seemed to fill the churchyard. Gabriel looked fearfully round—nothing was to be seen.

"What have you got in that bottle?" said the goblin.

"Gin, sir," replied the sexton, trembling more than ever.

"Who drinks gin alone, and in a churchyard, on such a night as this?" said the goblin.

"Gabriel Grub! Gabriel Grub!" exclaimed the wild voices again.

The goblin grinned maliciously at the terrified sexton and then, raising his voice, exclaimed: "And who, then, is our fair and lawful prize?"

To this inquiry the invisible chorus replied, in a strain that sounded like the voices of a choir singing to the mighty swell of the old church organ—a strain that seemed borne to the sexton's ears upon a wild wind, and to die away as it passed onward; but the reply was still the same: "Gabriel Grub! Gabriel Grub!"

The goblin grinned a broader grin than before, as he said, "Well Gabriel, what do you say to this?"

The sexton gasped for breath.

"What do you think of this, Gabriel?" said the goblin, kicking up his feet in the air on either side of the tombstone.

"It's—it's—very curious sir," replied the sexton, half dead with fright; "very curious, and very pretty, but I think I'll go back and finish my work, sir, if you please."

"Work!" said the goblin, "what work?"

"The grave, sir; making the grave," stammered the sexton.

"Oh, the grave, eh?" said the goblin. "Who makes graves at a time when all other men are merry, and takes pleasure in it?"

Again the mysterious voices replied, "Gabriel Grub! Gabriel Grub!"

"I'm afraid my friends want you, Gabriel," said the goblin, thrusting his tongue further into his cheek than ever—and a most astonishing tongue it was—"I'm afraid my friends want you, Gabriel," said the goblin.

"Please, sir," replied the horror-stricken sexton, "I don't think they can, sir. They don't know me, sir. I don't think the gentlemen have ever seen me, sir."

"Oh yes, they have," replied the goblin; "we know the man with the sulky face and grim scowl, that came down the street tonight, throwing his evil looks at the children, and grasping his burying spade the tighter. We know the man who struck the boy with envious malice of his heart because the boy could be merry, and he could not. We know him, we know him."

Here, the goblin gave a loud shrill laugh, which the echoes returned twenty-fold, and throwing his legs up in the air, stood upon his head, or rather upon the very point of his sugar-loaf hat, on the narrow edge of the tombstone. Then he threw a somersault with extraordinary agility, right to the sexton's feet.

"I—I—am afraid I must leave you, sir," said the sexton, making an effort to move.

"Leave us!" said the goblin, "Gabriel Grub going to leave us. Ho! ho! ho!"

As the goblin laughed, the sexton observed, for one instant, a brilliant illumination within the windows of the church, as if the whole building were lighted up. It disappeared, the organ pealed forth a lively air, and whole troops of goblins, perfect duplicates of the first one, poured into the churchyard and began playing at leap-frog with the tombstones, never stopping for an instant to take breath, but jumping the highest among them, one after the other, with the most marvelous dexterity. The first goblin was a most astonishing leaper, and none of the others could come near him; even in the extremity of his terror the sexton could not help observing that while his friends were content to leap over the common-sized gravestones, the first one took the family vaults, iron railings and all, with as much ease as if they had been so many streetposts.

At last the game reached a most exciting pitch; the organ played quicker and quicker; and the goblins leaped faster and faster, coiling themselves up, rolling head over heels upon the ground, and bounding over the tombstones like footballs. The sexton's brain whirled round with the rapidity of the motion he beheld, and his legs reeled beneath him as the spirits flew before his eyes. The goblin king, suddenly darting towards him, laid his hand upon his collar and sank with him through the earth.

When Gabriel Grub had had time to fetch his breath, which the rapidity of his descent had for the moment taken away, he found himself in what appeared to be a large cavern, surrounded on all sides by crowds of goblins ugly and grim. In the center of the room on an elevated seat was stationed his friend of the churchyard, and close beside stood Gabriel Grub himself, without power of motion.

"Cold tonight," said the king of the goblins, "very cold. A glass of something warm, here!"

At this command, half a dozen officious goblins, with a perpetual smile upon their faces, whom Gabriel Grub imagined to be courtiers, on that account hastily disappeared and presently returned with a goblet they presented to the king.

"Ah!" cried the goblin, whose cheeks and throat were transparent as he tossed down the flame. "This warms one, indeed! Bring a goblet of the same for Mr. Grub."

It did no good for the unfortunate sexton to protest that he was not in the habit of taking anything warm at night; one of the goblins held him while another poured the blazing liquid down his throat. The whole assembly screeched with laughter as he coughed and choked, and wiped away the tears which gushed plentifully from his eyes after swallowing the burning draught.

"And now," said the king, fantastically poking the tapered corner of his sugar-loaf hat into the sexton's eye and

thereby causing him the most exquisite pain, "And now, show the man of misery and gloom a few of the pictures from our own great storehouse!"

As the goblin said this, a thick cloud which obscured the remoter end of the cavern rolled gradually away and disclosed, at a great distance, a scantily furnished but neat and clean apartment. A crowd of little children were gathered round a bright fire, clinging to their mother's gown, and frolicking around her chair. The mother occasionally rose and drew aside the window curtain, as if to look for some expected object. A frugal meal was placed near the fire. A knock was heard at the door. The mother opened it, and the children crowded round her and clapped their hands for joy as their father entered. He was wet and weary, and shook the snow from his garments as the children crowded round him, and seizing his cloak, hat, stick and gloves, with busy zeal, ran with them from the room. Then, as he sat down to his meal before the fire, the children climbed about his knee and the mother sat by his side, and all seemed happiness and comfort.

But a change came upon the view, almost imperceptibly. The scene was altered to a small bedroom, where the fairest and youngest child lay dying; the rose had fled from his cheek and the light from his eye; even as the sexton looked upon him with an interest he had never felt or known before, he died. His young brothers and sisters crowded round his little bed and seized his tiny hand, so cold and heavy; but they shrunk back from its touch, and looked with awe on his infant face; for calm and tranquil as it was, and sleeping in rest and peace as the beautiful child seemed to be, they saw that he was dead, and they knew that he was an angel looking down upon and blessing them, from a bright and happy Heaven.

Again the light cloud passed across the picture, and again the subject changed. The father and mother were old and helpless now, and the number of those about them was diminished more than half; but content and cheerfulness sat on every face, and beamed in every eye, as they crowded round the fireside and told and listened to old stories of earlier and bygone days. Slowly and peacefully, the father sank into the grave, and soon after, the sharer of all his cares and troubles followed him to a place of rest. The few who yet survived them knelt by their tomb and watered the green turf which covered it with their tears; then rose, and turned away, sadly and mournfully, but not with bitter cries or despairing lamentations, for they knew that they should one day meet again. And once more they mixed with the busy world, and their content and cheerfulness was restored. The cloud settled upon the picture and concealed it from the sexton's view.

"What do you think of that?" said the goblin, turning his large face towards Gabriel Grub.

Gabriel murmured out something about its being very pretty, and looked somewhat ashamed, as the goblin bent his fiery eyes upon him.

"*You* a miserable man!" said the goblin, in a tone of excessive contempt. "You!" He appeared disposed to add more, but indignation choked his utterance so he lifted up one of his very pliable legs, and flourishing it above his head a little, to insure his aim, administered a good sound kick to

Gabriel Grub, immediately after which all the goblins in waiting crowded round the wretched sexton and kicked him without mercy.

"Show him some more!" said the king of the goblins.

At these words, the cloud was dispelled, and a rich and beautiful landscape was disclosed to view. The sun shone from out the clear blue sky, the water sparkled beneath his rays, and the trees looked greener, and the flowers more cheerful, beneath his cheering influence. The water rippled on with a pleasant sound; the trees rustled in the light wind that murmured among their leaves; the birds sang upon the boughs; and the lark caroled on high her welcome to the morning. Yes, it was morning; the bright, balmy morning of summer; the minutest leaf, the smallest blade of grass, was instilled with life. The ant crept forth to her daily toil, the butterfly fluttered and basked in the warm rays of the sun; myriads of insects spread their transparent wings, and reveled in their brief but happy existence; and all was brightness and splendor.

"You a miserable man!" said the king of the goblins, in a more contemptuous tone than before. And again the king of goblins gave his leg a twirl; again it descended on the shoulders of the sexton, and again the attendant goblins imitated the example of their chief.

Many a time the cloud went and came, and many a lesson it taught Gabriel Grub, who, although his shoulders pained from the frequent applications of the goblins' feet, looked on with an interest that nothing could diminish. He saw that men who worked hard and earned their scanty bread with lives of labor were cheerful and happy; and that to the most ignorant, the sweet face of nature was a never-failing source of cheerfulness and joy. He saw those who had been delicately nurtured, and tenderly brought up, cheerful under privation, and superior to suffering that would have crushed many of a rougher grain, because they bore within their own bosoms the materials of happiness, contentment, and peace. He saw that women, the tenderest and most fragile of God's creatures, were the oftenest superior to sorrow, adversity, and distress; and he saw that it was because they bore, in their own hearts, an inexhaustible well-spring of affection and devotion. Above all, he saw that men like himself, who snarled at the mirth and cheerfulness of others, were the foulest weeds on the fair surface of the earth; and setting all the good of the world against the evil, he came to the conclusion that it was a very decent and respectable sort of world after all. No sooner had he formed it, than the cloud which closed over the last picture seemed to settle on his senses and lull him to repose. One by one, the goblins faded from his sight. As the last one disappeared, he sunk to sleep.

The day had broken when Gabriel Grub awoke, and found himself lying at full length on the flat gravestone in the churchyard with the wicker bottle lying empty by his side, and his coat, spade, and lantern, all well whitened by the last night's frost, scattered on the ground. The stone on which he had first seen the goblin seated stood bolt upright before him, and the grave at which he had worked the night before was not far off. At first he began to doubt the reality of his adventures, but the acute pain in his shoulders when he attempted to rise, assured him that the kicking of the goblins was certainly not imaginary. He was staggered again by observing no traces of footsteps in the snow on which the goblins had played at leap-frog with the gravestones, but he speedily accounted for this circumstance when he remembered that, being spirits, they would leave no visible impression behind them. So, Gabriel Grub got on his feet as well as he could for the pain in his back, and brushing the frost off his coat, put it on, and turned his face towards the town.

But he was an altered man, and he could not bear the thought of returning to a place where his repentance would be scoffed at and his reformation disbelieved. He hesitated for a few moments, and then turned away to wander where he might, and seek his bread elsewhere.

The lantern, the spade, and the wicker bottle were found that day in the churchyard. There were a great many speculations about the sexton's fate at first, but it was speedily determined that he had been carried away by the goblins. At length this was devotedly believed.

Unfortunately, these stories were somewhat disturbed by the unlooked-for reappearance of Gabriel Grub himself, some ten years afterward, a ragged, contented, rheumatic old man. He told his story to the clergyman and also to the mayor, and in course of time it began to be received as a matter of history, in which form it has continued down to this very day. Some shrugged their shoulders, touched their foreheads, and murmured something about Gabriel Grub having drunk too much gin and then fallen asleep on the flat tombstone. They explained what he had witnessed in the goblin's cavern by saying that he had seen the world and grown wiser. But this opinion, which was not widely believed, gradually died off.

Be the matter how it may, this story has at least one moral if it teach no better one—and that is, that if a man turns sulky and drinks by himself at Christmas time, he may make up his mind to be not a bit the better for it. Let him beware the spirits which Gabriel Grub saw in the goblin's cavern.

THE CANTERVILLE GHOST
Oscar Wilde
(1856–1900)

With a name like Oscar Fingal O'Flahertie Wills Wilde, it's no wonder that Irish born Oscar Wilde was known for his "wild" and outrageous ways—both in his artistic and personal life. In fact, while still a student at Oxford, the young author wrote, "Somehow or other I'll be famous, and if not famous, I'll be notorious."

Wilde certainly lived up to his prediction. His notorious long wavy hair and fancy fur coats became just as famous as his writing. It was even reported that the flamboyant Wilde engaged in contests of loud dress with the American painter James Whistler.

Wilde's literary fame began at the age of 23, with the publication of some of his poetry. At 32, Wilde published his first collection of fiction, *The Happy Prince and Other Tales*; at 39, one of his most famous plays, *The Importance of Being Earnest*, was produced in London at the St. James Theater. Wilde often used his writing to challenge social conventions. This theme is particularly important in his most famous work, *The Picture of Dorian Gray*, a novel published in 1891.

Although he was once engaged to Bram Stoker's wife, Florence Balcombe, Wilde eventually married Constance Lloyd in 1883 and began raising a family. Unfortunately, as he grew older, Wilde's lifestyle became increasingly reckless—toward the end of his life he grew obese and drank excessively. Not surprisingly, his mind and body weakened to the point of exhaustion. Wilde died on November 30, 1900, at the young age of 44, of what most believe was a disease of the inner ear.

In this excerpt from the humorous and spooky story, "The Canterville Ghost," Wilde adds a new twist to the classic ghost story. You might ask yourself just who is scaring whom. Is it the family or the ghost who is the most frightened? You might also notice that the story pokes some fun at American values.

I

When Mr. Hiriam B. Otis, the American Minister, bought Canterville Chase, everyone told him he was doing a very foolish thing, as there was no doubt at all that the place was haunted. Indeed, Lord Canterville himself, who was a man of the most punctilious honor, had felt it his duty to mention the fact to Mr. Otis when they came to discuss terms.

"We have not cared to live in the place ourselves," said Lord Canterville, "since my grand-aunt, the Dowager Duchess of Bolton, was frightened into a fit, from which she never really recovered, by two skeleton hands being placed on her shoulders as she was dressing for dinner, and I feel bound to tell you, Mr. Otis, that the ghost has been seen by several living members of my family, as well as by the rector of the parish, the Rev. Augustus Dampier, who is a Fellow of King's College, Cambridge. After the unfortunate accident to the Duchess, none of our younger servants would stay with us, and Lady Canterville often got very little sleep at night, in consequence of the mysterious noises that came from the corridor and the library."

"My Lord," answered the Minister, "I will take the furniture and the ghost at a valuation. I come from a modern country, where we have everything that money can buy; and with all our spry young fellows painting the Old World red, and carrying off your best actresses and prima donnas, I reckon that if there were such a thing as a ghost in Europe, we'd have it at home in a very short time in one of our public museums, or on the road as a show."

"I fear that the ghost exists," said Lord Canterville, smiling, "though it may have resisted the overtures of your enterprising impresarios. It has been well known for three centuries, since 1584 in fact, and always makes its appearance before the death of any member of our family."

"Well, so does the family doctor, for that matter, Lord Canterville. But there is no such thing, sir, as a ghost, and I guess the laws of Nature are not going to be suspended for the British aristocracy."

"You are certainly very natural in America," answered Lord Canterville, who did not quite understand Mr. Otis's last observation, "and if you don't mind a ghost in the house, it is all right. Only you must remember I warned you."

A few weeks after this the purchase was completed, and at the close of the season, the Minister and his family went down to Canterville Chase. Mrs. Otis was a very handsome, middle-aged woman, with fine eyes, and a superb profile. Her eldest son, christened Washington by his parents in a moment of patriotism, which he never ceased to regret, was a fair-haired, rather good-looking young man. Miss Virginia E. Otis was a little girl of 15, lithe and lovely as a fawn, and with a fine freedom in her large, blue eyes. She was a wonderful amazon, and had once raced old Lord Bilton on her pony twice round the park, winning by a length and a half, just in front of the Achilles statue; to the huge delight of the young Duke of Cheshire, who proposed to her on the spot, and was sent back to Eton that very night by his guardians, in floods of tears. After Virginia came the twins. They were delightful boys, and, with the exception of the worthy Minister, the only true republicans of the family.

As Canterville Chase is seven miles from Ascot, the nearest railway station, Mr. Otis had telegraphed for a wagonette to meet them, and they started on their drive in high spirits. It was a lovely July evening, and the air was delicate with the scent of the pinewoods. As they entered the avenue of Canterville Chase, however, the sky became suddenly overcast with clouds, a curious stillness seemed to hold the atmosphere, a great flight of rooks passed silently over their heads, and, before they reached the house, some big drops of rain had fallen.

Standing on the steps to receive them was an old woman, neatly dressed in black silk, with a white cap and apron. This was Mrs. Umney, the housekeeper, whom Mrs. Otis, at Lady Canterville's earnest request, had consented to keep on in her former position. She made them each a low curtsy as they alighted, and said in a quaint, old-fashioned manner, "I bid you welcome to Canterville Chase." Following her, they passed through the fine Tudor hall into the library, a long, low room, paneled in black oak, at the end of which was a large stained-glass window. Here they found tea laid out for them, and, after taking off their wraps, they sat down and began to look around, while Mrs. Umney waited on them.

Suddenly Mrs. Otis caught sight of a dull red stain on the floor just by the fireplace and, quite unconscious of what it really signified, said to Mrs. Umney, "I am afraid something has been spilt there."

"Yes, madam," replied the housekeeper in a low voice, "blood has been spilt on that spot."

"How horrid," cried Mrs. Otis; "I don't at all care for blood-stains in a sitting-room. It must be removed at once."

The old woman smiled, and answered in the same low, mysterious voice, "It is the blood of Lady Eleanore de Canterville, who was murdered on that very spot by her own husband, Sir Simon de Canterville, in 1575. Sir Simon survived her nine years, and disappeared suddenly under very mysterious circumstances. His body has never been discovered, but his guilty spirit still haunts the Chase. The blood-stain has been much admired by tourists and others, and cannot be removed."

"That is all nonsense," cried Washington Otis; "Pinkerton's Champion Stain Remover and Paragon Detergent will clean it up in no time," and before the terrified housekeeper could interfere he had fallen upon his knees, and was rapidly scouring the floor with a small stick of what looked like a black cosmetic. In a few moments no trace of the bloodstain could be seen.

"I knew Pinkerton would do it," he exclaimed triumphantly, as he looked round at his admiring family; but no sooner had he said these words than a terrible flash of lightning lit up the somber room, a fearful peal of thunder made them all start to their feet, and Mrs. Umney fainted.

"My dear Hiram," cried Mrs. Otis, "what can we do with a woman who faints?"

"Charge it to her, like breakages," answered the Minister; "she won't faint after that"; and in a few moments Mrs. Umney certainly came to. There was no doubt, however, that she was extremely upset, and she sternly warned Mr. Otis to beware of some trouble coming to the house.

"I have seen things with my own eyes, sir," she said, "that would make any Christian's hair stand on end, and many and many a night I have not closed my eyes in sleep for the awful things that are done here." Mr. Otis, however, and his wife warmly assured the honest soul that they were not afraid of ghosts, and, after invoking the blessings of Providence on her new master and mistress, and making arrangements for an increase of salary, the old housekeeper tottered off to her own room.

II

The storm raged fiercely all that night, but nothing of particular note occurred. The next morning, however, when they came down to breakfast, they found the terrible stain of blood once again on the floor. "I don't think it can be the fault of the Paragon Detergent," said Washington, "for I have tried it with everything. It must be the ghost." He accordingly rubbed out the stain a second time, but the second morning it appeared again. The third morning also it was there, though the library had been locked up at night by Mr. Otis himself, and the key carried upstairs. The whole family was now quite interested; Mr. Otis began to suspect that he had been too dogmatic in his denial of the existence of ghosts, Mrs. Otis expressed her intention of joining the Psychical Society, and Washington prepared a long letter to Messrs. Myers and Podmore on the subject of the Permanence of Sanguineous Stains when connected with Crime. That night all doubts about the objective existence of phantasmata were removed forever.

The day had been warm and sunny; and, in the cool of the evening, the whole family went out for a drive. They did not return home till nine o'clock, when they had a light supper. No mention at all was made of the supernatural, nor was Sir Simon de Canterville alluded to in any way. At eleven o'clock the family retired, and by half-past all the lights were out. Some time after, Mr. Otis was awakened by a curious noise in the corridor, outside his room. It sounded like the clank of metal, and seemed to be coming nearer every moment. He got up at once, struck a match, and looked at the time. It was exactly one o'clock. He was quite calm, and felt his pulse, which was not at all feverish. The strange noise still continued, and with it he heard distinctly the sound of footsteps. He put on his slippers, took a small oblong phial out of his dressing-case, and opened the door.

Right in front of him he saw, in the wan moonlight, an old man of terrible aspect. His eyes were as red as burning coals; his garments, which were of antique cut, were soiled and ragged and from his wrists and ankles hung heavy manacles and rusty gyves.

"My dear sir," said Mr. Otis, "I really must insist on your oiling those chains, and have brought you for that purpose a small bottle of the Tammany Rising Sun Lubricator. I shall leave it here for you by the bedroom candles, and will be happy to supply you with more should you require it." With these words the United States Minister laid the bottle down on a marble table, and, closing his door, retired to rest.

For a moment the Canterville ghost stood quite motionless in natural indignation; then, dashing the bottle violently upon the polished floor, he fled down the corridor, uttering hollow groans, and emitting a ghastly green light. Just, however, as he reached the top of the great oak staircase, a door was flung open, two little white-robed figures appeared, and a large pillow whizzed past his head! There was evidently no time to be lost, so, hastily adopting the Fourth Dimension of Space as a means of escape, he vanished through the wainscoting, and the house became quite quiet.

On reaching a small, secret chamber in the left wing, he leaned up against a moonbeam to recover his breath, and began to try and realize his position. Never, in a brilliant and uninterrupted career of three hundred years, had he been so grossly insulted. He thought of the Dowager Duchess, whom he had frightened into a fit as she stood before the glass in her lace and diamonds, and of old Madame de Tremouillac, who, having wakened up one morning early and seen a skeleton

seated in an arm-chair by the fire reading her diary, had been
confined to her bed for six weeks with an attack of brain
fever, and, on her recovery, had become reconciled to the
Church, and broken off her connection with that notorious
skeptic Monsieur de Voltaire. He remembered the terrible
night when the wicked Lord Canterville was found choking
in his dressing-room, with a knave of diamonds halfway
down his throat, and confessed, just before he died, that he
had cheated Charles James Fox out of £50,000 at Crockford's
by means of that very card, and swore that the ghost had
made him swallow it. With the enthusiastic egotism of the
true artist he went over his most celebrated performances,
and smiled bitterly to himself as he recalled to mind his last
appearance as "Red Ruben, or the Strangled Babe," his debut
as "Gaunt Gibeon, the Blood-sucker of Bexley Moor," and
the furor he had excited, one lovely June evening, by merely
playing ninepins with his own bones upon the lawn-tennis
ground. And after all this, some wretched modern Americans were to come and offer him the Rising Sun Lubricator,
and throw pillows at his head! It was quite unbearable. Besides, no ghosts in history had ever been treated in this manner. Accordingly, he determined to have vengeance, and
remained till daylight in an attitude of deep thought.

III

The next morning when the Otis family met at breakfast,
they discussed the ghost at some length. The United States
Minister was naturally a little annoyed to find that his present had not been accepted. "I have no wish," he said, "to do

the ghost any personal injury, and I must say that, considering the length of time he has been in the house, I don't think it is at all polite to throw pillows at him"—a very just remark, at which, I am sorry to say, the twins burst into shouts of laughter. "Upon the other hand," he continued, "if he really declines to use the Rising Sun Lubricator, we shall have to take his chains from him. It would be quite impossible to sleep with such a noise going on outside the bedrooms."

For the rest of the week, however, they were undisturbed, the only thing that excited any attention being the continual renewal of the bloodstain on the library floor. This certainly was very strange, as the door was always locked at night by Mr. Otis, and the windows kept closely barred. The chameleon-like color, also, of the stain excited a good deal of comment. Some mornings it was a dull (almost Indian) red, then it would be vermilion, then a rich purple, and once when they came down for family prayers, they found it a bright emerald-green. These kaleidoscopic changes naturally amused the party very much, and bets on the subject were freely made every evening. The only person who did not enter into the joke was little Virginia, who, for some unexplained reason, was always a good deal distressed at the sight of the bloodstain, and very nearly cried the morning it was emerald-green.

The second appearance of the ghost was on Sunday night. Shortly after they had gone to bed they were suddenly alarmed by a fearful crash in the hall. Rushing downstairs, they found that a large suit of old armor had become detached from its stand, and had fallen on the stone floor, while seated in a high-backed chair was the Canterville ghost, rubbing his knees with an expression of acute agony on his face. The twins, having brought their pea-shooters with them, at once discharged two pellets at him with that accuracy of aim which can only be attained by long and careful practice on a writing-master, while the United States Minister covered him with his revolver, and called upon him, in accordance with Californian etiquette, to hold up his hands! The ghost started up with a wild shriek of rage, and swept through them like a mist, extinguishing Washington Otis's candle as he passed, and so leaving them all in total darkness. On reaching the top of the staircase he recovered himself, and determined to give his celebrated peal of demoniac laughter. This he had on more than one occasion found extremely useful. It was said to have turned Lord Raker's wig gray in a single night, and had certainly made three of Lady Canterville's French governesses give warning before their month was up. He accordingly laughed his most horrible laugh, till the old vaulted roof rang and rang again, but hardly had the fearful echo died away when a door opened, and Mrs. Otis came out in a light blue dressing-gown. "I am afraid you are far from well," she said, "and have brought you a bottle of Dr. Dobell's tincture. If it is indigestion, you will find it a most excellent remedy." The ghost glared at her in fury, and began at once to make preparations for turning himself into a large black dog, an accomplishment for which he was justly renowned, and to which the family doctor always attributed the permanent idiocy of Lord Canterville's uncle, the Hon. Thomas Horton. The sound of approaching footsteps, however, made him hesitate in his fell purpose, so he contented himself with becoming faintly phosphorescent, and vanished with a deep, churchyard groan, just as the twins had come up to him.

On reaching his room he entirely broke down, and became a prey to the most violent agitation. The vulgarity of the twins, and the gross materialism of Mrs. Otis, were naturally extremely annoying, but what really distressed him most was, that he had been unable to wear the suit of mail. He had hoped that even modern Americans would be thrilled by the sight of a Specter In Armor, if for no more sensible reason, at least out of respect for their national poet, Longfellow, over whose graceful and attractive poetry he himself had whiled away many a weary hour when the Cantervilles were up in town. Besides, it was his own suit. He had worn it with great success at the Kenilworth tournament, and had been highly complimented on it by no less a person than the Virgin Queen herself. Yet when he had put it on he had been completely overpowered by the weight of the huge breastplate and steel casque, and had fallen heavily on the stone pavement.

For some days after this he was extremely ill, and hardly stirred out of his room at all, except to keep the bloodstain in proper repair. However, by taking great care of himself, he recovered, and resolved to make a third attempt to frighten the United States Minister and his family. His plan of action was this. He was to make his way quietly to Washington Otis's room, gibber at him from the foot of the bed, and stab himself three times in the throat to the sound of slow music. He bore Washington a special grudge, being quite aware that it was he who was in the habit of removing the famous Canterville bloodstain, by means of Pinkerton's

Paragon Detergent. Having reduced the reckless and fool-hardy youth to a condition of abject terror, he was then to proceed to the room occupied by the United States Minister and his wife, and there to place a clammy hand on Mrs. Otis's forehead, while he hissed into her trembling husband's ear the awful secrets of the charnel-house. With regard to little Virginia, he had not quite made up his mind. She had never insulted him in any way, and was pretty and gentle. A few hollow groans from the wardrobe, he thought, would be more than sufficient, or, if that failed to wake her, he might grabble at the counterpane with palsy-twitching fingers. As for the twins, he was quite determined to teach them a lesson. The first thing to be done was, of course, to sit upon their chests, so as to produce the stifling sensation of nightmare. Then, as their beds were quite close to each other, to stand between them in the form of a green, icy-cold corpse, till they became paralyzed with fear, and finally, to throw off the winding-sheet, and crawl round the room, with white, bleached bones and one rolling eyeball.

At half-past 10 he heard the family going to bed. For some time he was disturbed by wild shrieks of laughter from the twins, who, with the light-hearted gaiety of school-boys, were evidently amusing themselves before they retired to rest, but at a quarter past 11 all was still, and, as midnight sounded, he sallied forth. The owl beat against the window panes, the raven croaked from the old yew tree, and the wind wandered moaning round the house like a lost soul; but the Otis family slept unconscious of their doom, and high above the rain and storm he could hear the steady snoring of the Minister for the United States. He stepped stealthily out of the wainscoting, with an evil smile on his cruel, wrinkled mouth, and the moon hid her face in a cloud as he stole past the great oriel window, where his own arms and those of his murdered wife were blazoned in azure and gold. On and on he glided, like an evil shadow, the very darkness seeming to loathe him as he passed. Finally he reached the corner of the passage that led to luckless Washington's room. For a moment he paused there, the wind blowing his long gray locks about his head, and twisting into grotesque and fantastic folds the nameless horror of the dead man's shroud. Then the clock struck the quarter, and he felt the time was come. He chuckled to himself, and turned the corner; but no sooner had he done so, than, with a piteous wail of terror, he fell back, and hid his blanched face in his long, bony hands. Right in front of him was standing a horrible specter, motionless as a carven image, and monstrous as a madman's dream! On its breast was a placard with strange writing in antique characters, some scroll of shame it seemed, some record of wild sins, some awful calendar of crime, and, with its right hand, it bore aloft a falchion of gleaming steel.

Never having seen a ghost before, he naturally was terribly frightened, and, after a second hasty glance at the awful phantom, he fled back to his room, tripping up in his long winding-sheet as he sped down the corridor, and finally dropping the rusty dagger into the Minister's jackboots, where it was found in the morning by the butler. Once in the privacy of his own apartment, he flung himself down on a small pallet-bed, and hid his face under the clothes. After a time, however, the brave old Canterville spirit asserted itself, and he determined to go and speak to the other ghost as soon as it was daylight. Accordingly, just as the dawn was touching the hills with silver, he returned towards the spot where he had first laid eyes on the grisly phantom, feeling that, after all, two ghosts were better than one, and that, by the aid of his new friend, he might safely grapple with the twins. On reaching the spot, however, a terrible sight met his gaze. Something had evidently happened to the specter, for the light had entirely faded from its hollow eyes, the gleaming falchion had fallen from its hand, and it was leaning up against the wall in a strained and uncomfortable attitude. He rushed forward and seized it in his arms, when, to his horror, the head slipped off and rolled on the floor, the body assumed a recumbent posture, and he found himself clasping a white dimity bed-curtain, with a sweeping-brush, a kitchen cleaver, and a hollow turnip lying at his feet! Unable to understand this curious transformation, he clutched the placard with feverish haste, and there, in the gray morning light, he read these fearful words:

YE OTIS GHOST.
YE ONLIE TRUE AND ORIGINALE SPOOK,
BEWARE OF YE IMITATIONES.
ALL OTHERS ARE COUNTERFEITS.

The whole thing flashed across him. He had been tricked, foiled, and outwitted! The old Canterville look came into his eyes; he ground his toothless gums together; and, raising his withered hands high above his head, swore, according to the picturesque phraseology of the antique school, that when

Chanticleer had sounded twice his merry horn, deeds of blood would be wrought, and Murder walk abroad with silent feet.

Hardly had he finished this awful oath when, from the red-tiled roof of a distant homestead, a cock crew. He laughed a long, low, bitter laugh, and waited. Hour after hour he waited, but the cock, for some strange reason, did not crow again. Finally, at half-past seven, the arrival of the housemaids made him give up his fearful vigil, and he stalked back to his room, thinking of his vain hope and baffled purpose. There he consulted several books on ancient chivalry, of which he was exceedingly fond, and found that, on every occasion on which his oath had been used, Chanticleer had always crowed a second time. "Perdition seize the naughty fowl," he muttered. "I have seen the day when, with my stout spear, I would have run him through the gorge, and made him crow for me an 'twere in death!" He then retired to a comfortable lead coffin, and stayed there till evening.

IV

The next day the ghost was very weak and tired. The terrible excitement of the last four weeks was beginning to have its effect. His nerves were completely shattered, and he started at the slightest noise. For five days he kept to his room, and at last made up his mind to give up the point of the bloodstain on the library floor. If the Otis family did not want it, they clearly did not deserve it. The question of phantasmic apparitions, and the development of astral bodies, was, of course, quite a different matter, and really not under his control. It was his solemn duty to appear in the corridor once a week, and to gibber from the large oriel window on the first and third Wednesday in every month, and he did not see how he could honorably escape from his obligations. It is quite true that his life had been very evil, but, upon the other hand, he was most conscientious in all things connected with the supernatural. For the next three Saturdays, accordingly, he traversed the corridor as usual between midnight and three o'clock, taking every possible precaution against being either heard or seen. He removed his boots, trod as lightly as possible on the old, worm-eaten boards, wore a large black velvet cloak, and was careful to use the Rising Sun Lubricator for oiling his chains. He felt a little humiliated at first, but afterwards was sensible enough to see that there was a great deal to be said for the invention, and, to a certain degree, it served his purpose. Still, in spite of everything, he was not left unmolested. He now gave up all hope of ever frightening this rude American family, and contented himself, as a rule, with creeping about the passages in slippers, with a thick red muffler round his throat for fear of draughts, and a small arquebus, in case he should be attacked by the twins. The final blow he received occurred on the 19th of September. It was about a quarter past two o'clock in the morning, and, as far as he could ascertain, no one was stirring. As he was strolling towards the library, however, to see if there were any traces left of the bloodstain, suddenly there leaped out on him from a dark corner two figures, who waved their arms wildly above their heads, and shrieked out "BOO!" in his ear.

Seized with a panic, which, under the circumstances, was only natural, he rushed for the staircase, but found Washington Otis waiting for him there with the big garden-syringe; and being thus hemmed in by his enemies on every side, and driven almost to bay, he vanished into the great iron stove, which, fortunately for him, was not lit, and had to make his way home through the flues and chimneys, arriving at his own room in a terrible state of dirt, disorder, and despair.

After this he was not seen again on any nocturnal expedition. It was generally assumed that the ghost had gone away, and, in fact, Mr. Otis wrote a letter to that effect to Lord Canterville, who, in reply, expressed his great pleasure at the news, and sent his best congratulations to the Minister's worthy wife.

The Otises, however, were deceived, for the ghost was still in the house, and, though now almost an invalid, was by no means ready to let the matter rest, particularly as he heard that among the guests was the young Duke of Cheshire, whose grand-uncle, Lord Francis Stilton, had once bet a hundred guineas with Colonel Carbury that he would play dice with the Canterville ghost, and was found the next morning lying on the floor of the card-room in such a helpless paralytic state, that though he lived on to a great age, he was never able to say anything again but "Double Sixes." The ghost, then, was naturally very anxious to show that he had not lost his influence over the Stiltons, with whom, as everyone knows, the Dukes of Cheshire are lineally descended. Accordingly, he made arrangement for appearing to Virginia's little lover in his celebrated impersonation of "The Vampire Monk, or the Bloodless Benedictine." At the last moment, however, his terror of the twins prevented his leaving his room, and the little Duke slept in peace under the great feathered canopy in the Royal Bed-chamber, and dreamed of Virginia.

V

A few days after this, Virginia and her curly-haired cavalier went out riding on Brockley meadows, where she tore her habit so badly in getting through a hedge, that, on her return home, she made up her mind to go up by the back staircase so as not to be seen. As she was running past the Tapestry Chamber, the door of which happened to be open, she fancied she saw someone inside, and thinking it was her mother's maid, who sometimes used to bring her work there, looked in to ask her to mend her habit. To her immense surprise, however, it was the Canterville Ghost himself! His head was leaning on his hand, and his whole attitude was one of extreme depression. Indeed, so forlorn, and so much out of repair did he look, that little Virginia, whose first idea had been to run away and lock herself in her room, was filled with pity, and determined to try to comfort him. So light was her footfall, and so deep his melancholy, that he was not aware of her presence until she spoke to him.

"I am so sorry for you," she said, "but my brothers are going back to Eton tomorrow, and then, if you behave yourself, no one will annoy you."

"It is absurd asking me to behave myself," he answered, looking round in astonishment at the pretty little girl who had ventured to address him, "quite absurd. I must rattle my chains, and groan through keyholes, and walk about at night, if that is what you mean. It is my only reason for existing."

"It is no reason at all for existing, and you know you have been very wicked. Mrs. Umney told us, the first day we arrived here, that you had killed your wife."

"Well, I quite admit it," said the Ghost petulantly, "but it was a purely family matter, and concerned no one else."

"It is very wrong to kill anyone," said Virginia, who at times had a sweet Puritan gravity, caught from some old New England ancestor.

"Oh, I hate the cheap severity of abstract ethics! My wife was very plain, never had my ruffs properly starched, and knew nothing about cookery. Why, there was a buck I had shot in Hogley Woods, a magnificent pricket, and do you know how she had it sent up to table? However, it is no matter now, for it is all over, and I don't think it was very nice of her brothers to starve me to death, though I did kill her."

"Starve you to death? Oh, Mr. Ghost, I mean Sir Simon, are you hungry? I have a sandwich in my case. Would you like it?"

"No, thank you, I never eat anything now; but it is very kind of you, all the same, and you are much nicer than the rest of your horrid, rude, vulgar, dishonest family."

"Stop!" cried Virginia, stamping her foot, "it is you who are rude, and horrid, and vulgar, and as for dishonesty, you know you stole the paints out of my box to try and furbish up that ridiculous bloodstain in the library. First you took all my reds, including the vermilion, and I couldn't do any more sunsets, and then you took the emerald-green and the chrome-yellow, and finally I had nothing left but indigo and Chinese white, and could only do moonlight scenes, which are always depressing to look at, and not at all easy to paint.

I never told on you, though I was very much annoyed, and it was most ridiculous, the whole thing; for who ever heard of emerald-green blood?"

"Well, really," said the Ghost, rather meekly, "what was I to do? It is a very difficult thing to get real blood nowadays, and, as your brother began it all with his Paragon Detergent, I certainly saw no reason why I should not have your paints. As for color, that is always a matter of taste; the Cantervilles have blue blood, for instance, the very bluest in England; but I know you Americans don't care for things of this kind."

"You know nothing about it, and the best thing you can do is to emigrate and improve your mind. My father will be only too happy to give you a free passage, and though there is a heavy duty on spirits of every kind, there will be no difficulty about the Custom House, as the officers are all Democrats. Once in New York, you are sure to be a great success. I know lots of people there who would give a hundred thousand dollars to have a grandfather, and much more than that to have a family Ghost."

"I don't think I should like America."

"I suppose because we have no ruins and no curiosities," said Virginia satirically.

"No ruins! No curiosities!" answered the Ghost; "you have your navy and your manners."

"Good evening; I will go and ask papa to get the twins an extra week's holiday."

"Please don't go, Miss Virginia," he cried; "I am so lonely and so unhappy, and I really don't know what to do. I want to go to sleep and I cannot."

"That's quite absurd! You have merely to go to bed and blow out the candle. It is very difficult, sometimes, to keep awake, especially at church, but there is no difficulty at all about sleeping. Why, even babies know how to do that, and they are not very clever."

"I have not slept for three hundred years," he said sadly, and Virginia's beautiful blue eyes opened in wonder; "for three hundred years I have not slept, and I am so tired."

Virginia grew quite grave, and her little lips trembled like rose-leaves. She came toward him, and kneeling down at his side, looked up into his old, withered face.

"Poor, poor Ghost," she murmured; "have you no place where you can sleep?"

"Far away beyond the pine-woods," he answered, in a low dreamy voice, "there is a little garden. There the grass grows long and deep, there are the great white stars of the hemlock flower, there the nightingale sings all night long. All night long he sings, and the cold, crystal moon looks down, and the yew tree spreads out its giant arms over the sleepers."

Virginia's eyes grew dim with tears, and she hid her face in her hands. "You mean the Garden of Death," she whispered.

"Yes, Death. Death must be so beautiful. To lie in the soft, brown earth, with the grasses waving above one's head, and listen to silence. To have no yesterday, and no tomorrow. To forget time, to forgive life, to be at peace. You can help me. You can open for me the portals of Death's house, for Love is always with you, and Love is stronger than Death is."

Virginia trembled, a cold shudder ran through her, and for a few moments there was silence. She felt as if she was in a terrible dream.

Then the Ghost spoke again. "Have you ever read the old prophecy on the library window?"

"Oh, often," cried the little girl, looking up; "I know it quite well. It is painted in curious black letters, and it is difficult to read. There are only six lines:

When a golden girl can win
Prayer from out of the lips of sin,
When the barren almond bears,
And a little child gives away its tears,
Then shall all the house be still
And peace come to Canterville.

"But I don't know what they mean."

"They mean," he said sadly, "that you must weep for me for my sins, because I have no tears, and pray with me for my soul, because I have no faith, and then, if you have always been sweet, and good, and gentle, the Angel of Death will have mercy on me."

Virginia made no answer, and the Ghost wrung his hands in wild despair as he looked down at her bowed golden head. Suddenly she stood up, very pale, and with a strange light in her eyes. "I am not afraid," she said firmly, "and I will ask the Angel to have mercy on you."

He rose from his seat with a faint cry of joy, and taking her hand bent over it with old-fashioned grace and kissed it.

His fingers were as cold as ice, and his lips burned like fire, but Virginia did not falter, as he led her across the dusky room. On the faded green tapestry were embroidered little huntsmen. They blew their tasseled horns, and with their tiny hands waved to her to go back. "Go back! little Virginia," they cried, "go back!" but the Ghost clutched her hand more tightly, and she shut her eyes against them. Horrible animals with lizard tails, and goggle eyes, blinked at her from the carven chimneypiece, and murmured, "Beware! little Virginia, beware! we may never see you again," but the Ghost glided on more swiftly, and Virginia did not listen. When they reached the end of the room he stopped, and muttered some words she could not understand. She opened her eyes, and saw the wall slowly fading away like a mist, and a great black cavern in front of her. A bitter cold wind swept round them, and she felt something pulling at her dress. "Quick, quick," cried the Ghost, "or it will be too late," and, in a moment, the wainscoting had closed behind them, and the Tapestry Chamber was empty.

VI

About 10 minutes later the bell rang for tea, and, as Virginia did not come down, Mrs. Otis sent up one of the footmen to tell her. After a little time he returned and said that he could not find Miss Virginia anywhere. As she was in the habit of going out to the garden every evening to get flowers for the dinner-table, Mrs. Otis was not at all alarmed at first, but when six o'clock struck, and Virginia did not appear, she became really agitated, and sent the boys out to look for her while she herself and Mr. Otis searched every room in the house. At half-past six the boys came back and said that they could find no trace of their sister anywhere. They were all now in the greatest state of excitement, and did not know what to do, when Mr. Otis suddenly remembered that, some few days before, he had given a band of gypsies permission to camp in the park. He accordingly at once set off for Blackfell Hollow, where he knew they were, accompanied by his eldest son and two of the farm-servants. The little Duke of Cheshire, who was perfectly frantic with anxiety, begged hard to be allowed to go too, but Mr. Otis would not allow him, as he was afraid there might be a scuffle. On arriving at the spot, however, he found that the gypsies had gone, and it was evident that their departure had been rather sudden, as the fire was still burning, and some plates were lying on the grass. Having sent off Washington and the two men to scour the district, he ran home, and dispatched telegrams to all the police inspectors in the county, telling them to look out for a little girl who had been kidnapped by tramps or gypsies. He then ordered his horse to be brought round, and after insisting on his wife and the three boys sitting down to dinner, rode off down the Ascot Road with a groom. He had hardly, however, gone a couple of miles when he heard somebody galloping after him, and, looking round, saw the little Duke coming up on his pony, with his face very flushed and no hat. "I'm awfully sorry, Mr. Otis," gasped out the boy, "but I can't eat any dinner as long as Virginia is lost. Please, don't be angry with me; if you had let us be engaged last year there would never have been all this trouble. You won't send me back, will you? I can't go! I won't go!"

The Minister could not help smiling at the handsome young scapegrace, and was a good deal touched at his devotion to Virginia, so leaning down from his horse, he patted him kindly on the shoulders, and said, "Well, Cecil, if you won't go back I suppose you must come with me, but I must get you a hat at Ascot."

"Oh, bother my hat! I want Virginia!" cried the little Duke, laughing, and they galloped on to the railway station. There Mr. Otis inquired of the stationmaster if anyone answering the description of Virginia had been seen on the platform, but could get no news of her. The stationmaster, however, wired up and down the line, and assured him that a strict watch would be kept for her, and, after having bought a hat for the little Duke from a linen draper, who was just putting up his shutters, Mr. Otis rode off to Bexley, a village about four miles away, which he was told was a well-known haunt of the gypsies, as there was a large common next to it. Here they roused up the rural policeman, but could get no information from him, and, after riding all over the common, they turned their horses' heads homewards, and reached the Chase about 11 o'clock, dead-tired and almost heart-broken. They found Washington and the twins waiting for them at the gate-house with lanterns, as the avenue was very dark. Not the slightest trace of Virginia had been discovered. The gypsies had been caught on Brockley meadows, but she was not with them, and they had explained their sudden departure by saying that they had mistaken the date of Chorton Fair, and had gone off in a hurry for fear they might be late. Indeed, they had been quite distressed at hearing of Virginia's disappearance, as

151

they were very grateful to Mr. Otis for having allowed them to camp in his park, and four of their number had stayed behind to help in the search. The carp-pond had been dragged, and the whole Chase thoroughly gone over, but without any result. It was evident that, for that night, at any rate, Virginia was lost to them; and it was in a state of the deepest depression that Mr. Otis and the boys walked up to the house, the groom following behind with the two horses and the pony. In the hall they found a group of frightened servants, and lying on a sofa in the library was poor Mrs. Otis, almost out of her mind with terror and anxiety, and having her forehead bathed with eau-de-cologne by the old housekeeper. Mr. Otis at once insisted on her having something to eat, and ordered up supper for the whole party. It was a melancholy meal, as hardly anyone spoke, and even the twins were awe-struck, and subdued, as they were very fond of their sister. When they had finished, Mr. Otis, in spite of the entreaties of the little Duke, ordered them all to bed, saying that nothing more could be done that night, and that he would telegraph in the morning to Scotland Yard for some detectives to be sent down immediately. Just as they were passing out of the dining-room, midnight began to boom from the clock-tower, and when the last stroke sounded they heard a crash and a sudden shrill cry; a dreadful peal of thunder shook the house, a strain of unearthly music floated through the air, a panel at the top of the staircase flew back with a loud noise, and out on the landing, looking very pale and white, with a little casket in her hand, stepped Virginia. In a moment they had all rushed up to her. Mrs. Otis clasped her passionately in her arms, the Duke smothered her with violent kisses, and the twins executed a wild war-dance round the group.

"Good heavens, child! Where have you been?" said Mr. Otis, rather angrily, thinking that she had been playing some foolish trick on them. "Cecil and I have been riding all over the country looking for you, and your mother has been frightened to death. You must never play these practical jokes anymore."

"Except on the Ghost! except on the Ghost!" shrieked the twins, as they capered about.

"My own darling, thank God you are found, you must never leave my side again," murmured Mrs. Otis, as she kissed the trembling child, and smoothed the tangled gold of her hair.

"Papa," said Virginia quietly, "I have been with the Ghost. He is dead, and you must come and see him. He had been very wicked, but he was really sorry for all that he had done, and he gave me this box of beautiful jewels before he died."

The whole family gazed at her in mute amazement, but she was quite grave and serious; and, turning round, she led them through the opening in the wainscoting down a narrow secret corridor, Washington following with a lighted candle, which he had caught up from the table. Finally, they came to a great oak door, studded with rusty nails. When Virginia touched it, it swung back on its heavy hinges, and they found themselves in a little, low room, with a vaulted ceiling, and one tiny grated window. Imbedded in the wall was a huge iron ring, and chained to it was a gaunt skeleton, that was stretched out at full length on the stone floor, and seemed to be trying to grasp with its long, fleshless fingers an old-fashioned trencher and ewer, that were placed just out of its reach. The jug had evidently been once filled with water, as it was covered with green mould. There was nothing on the trencher but a pile of dust. Virginia knelt down beside the skeleton, and, folding her little hands together, began to pray silently, while the rest of the party looked on in wonder at the terrible tragedy whose secret was now disclosed to them.

"Hallo!" suddenly exclaimed one of the twins, who had been looking out of the window trying to discover in what wing of the house the room was situated. "Hallo! the old withered almond-tree has blossomed. I can see the flowers quite plainly in the moonlight."

"God has forgiven him," said Virginia gravely, as she rose to her feet, and a beautiful light seemed to illumine her face.

"What an angel you are!" cried the young Duke, and he put his arm around her neck and kissed her.

A RAID ON THE
OYSTER PIRATES

Jack London
(1876–1916)

JACK LONDON had a difficult time growing up. His family was poor, and London was in trouble at an early age. He became an oyster pirate and gang leader before running away at the age of 17 to become a sailor. In his 20s he began aimlessly wandering the United States and Canada. It took a 30-day jail sentence to motivate the young man to change. London worked his way through high school and started college only to leave in 1897 to hunt for gold in the Klondike region of Alaska.

Not finding any gold, Jack London began writing to earn some money. He wrote adventurous tales based on his own experiences growing up in California and exploring in Canada and Alaska. He claimed his success came from hard work—he completed more than 50 books between 1900 and 1916, not to mention hundreds of short stories and countless articles on a wide range of subjects. London also possessed a remarkable talent for bringing an unfamiliar setting to life. In his most well-known books, *The Call of the Wild* and *White Fang*, the wilderness is described so clearly you feel transported, able

to see the distant mountains, smell the sap of the pine trees, feel the snow sting your cheeks, and hear the howling of the wind. Let "A Raid on the Oyster Pirates" carry you into the world of the fishermen, pirates, and patrolmen who inhabited the San Francisco Bay in 1905.

Of the fish patrolmen under whom we served at various times, Charley Le Grant and I were agreed, I think, that Neil Partington was the best. He was neither dishonest nor cowardly; and while he demanded strict obedience when we were under his orders, at the same time our relations were those of easy comradeship, and he permitted us a freedom to which we were ordinarily unaccustomed, as the present story will show.

Neil's family lived in Oakland, which is on the Lower Bay, not more than six miles across the water from San Francisco. One day, while scouting among the Chinese shrimp catchers of Point Pedro, he received word that his wife was very ill.

Within the hour the *Reindeer* was bowling along for Oakland, with a stiff northwest breeze astern. We ran up the Oakland Estuary and came to anchor, and in the days that followed, while Neil was ashore, we tightened up the Reindeer's rigging, overhauled the ballast, scraped down, and put the sloop into thorough shape.

This done, time hung heavy on our hands. Neil's wife was dangerously ill, and the outlook was a week's lie-over, awaiting the crisis. Charley and I roamed the docks, wondering what we should do, and so came upon the oyster fleet lying at the Oakland city wharf. In the main they were trim, natty boats, made for speed and bad weather, and we sat down on the stringpiece of the dock to study them.

"A good catch, I guess," Charley said, pointing to the heaps of oysters, assorted in three sizes, which lay upon their decks.

Peddlers were backing their wagons to the edge of the wharf, and from the bargaining and chaffering that went on, I managed to learn the selling price of the oysters.

"That boat must have at least $200 worth aboard," I calculated. "I wonder how long it took to get the load?"

"Three or four days," Charley answered. "Not bad wages for two men—$25 a day apiece."

The boat we were discussing, the *Ghost*, lay directly beneath us. Two men comprised its crew. One was a squat, broad-shouldered fellow with remarkably long and gorilla-like arms, while the other was tall and well proportioned, with clear blue eyes and a mat of straight black hair. So unusual and striking was this combination of hair and eyes that Charley and I remained somewhat longer than we intended.

And it was well that we did. A stout, elderly man with the dress and carriage of a successful merchant came up and stood beside us, looking down upon the deck of the *Ghost*. He appeared angry, and the longer he looked the angrier he grew.

"Those are my oysters," he said at last. "I know they are my oysters. You raided my beds last night and robbed me of them."

The tall man and the short man on the *Ghost* looked up.

"Hello, Taft," the short man said, with insolent familiarity. (Among the bay farers he had gained the nickname of "the Centipede" on account of his long arms.) "Hello, Taft," he repeated, with the same touch of insolence. "What're you growling about now?"

"Those are my oysters. That's what I said. You've stolen them from my beds."

"Yer mighty wise, ain't ye?" was the Centipede's sneering reply. "S'pose you can tell your oysters wherever you see 'em?"

"Now, in my experience," broke in the tall man, "oysters is oysters wherever you find 'em, and they're pretty much alike all the Bay over, and the world over, too, for that matter. We're not wanting to quarrel with you, Mr. Taft, but we just wish you wouldn't insinuate that them oysters is yours and that we're thieves and robbers till you can prove the goods."

"I know they're mine. I'd stake my life on it!" Mr. Taft snorted.

"Prove it," challenged the tall man, who we afterward learned was known as "the Porpoise" because of his wonderful swimming abilities.

Mr. Taft shrugged his shoulders helplessly. Of course, he could not prove the oysters to be his, no matter how certain he might be.

"I'd give $1,000 to have you men behind the bars!" he cried. "I'll give $50 a head for your arrest and conviction, all of you!"

A roar of laughter went up from the different boats, for the rest of the pirates had been listening to the discussion.

"There's more money in oysters," the Porpoise remarked dryly.

Mr. Taft turned impatiently on his heel and walked away. From out of the corner of his eye, Charley noted the way he went. Several minutes later, when he had disappeared around a corner, Charley rose lazily to his feet. I followed him, and we sauntered off in the opposite direction to that taken by Mr. Taft.

"Come on! Lively!" Charley whispered, when we passed from the view of the oyster fleet.

Our course was changed at once, and we dodged around corners and raced up and down sidestreets till Mr. Taft's generous form loomed up ahead of us.

"I'm going to interview him about that reward," Charley explained, as we rapidly overhauled the oyster-bed owner. "Neil will be delayed here for a week, and you and I might as well be doing something in the meantime. What do you say?"

"Of course, of course," Mr. Taft said, when Charley had introduced himself and explained his errand. "Those thieves are robbing me of thousands of dollars every year, and I shall be glad to break them up at any price, yes, sir, at any price. As I said, I'll give $50 a head and call it cheap at that. They've robbed my beds, torn down my signs, terrorized my watchmen, and last year killed one of them. Couldn't prove it. All done in the blackness of night. All I had was a dead watchman and no evidence. The detectives could do nothing. Nobody has been able to do anything with those men. We have never succeeded in arresting one of them. So I say, Mr.—what did you say your name was?"

"Le Grant," Charley answered.

"So I say, Mr. Le Grant, I am deeply obliged to you for the

assistance you offer. And I shall be glad, most glad, sir, to co-operate with you in every way. My watchmen and boats are at your disposal. Come and see me at the San Francisco offices anytime, or telephone at my expense. And don't be afraid of spending money. I'll foot your expenses, whatever they are, so long as they are within reason. The situation is growing desperate, and something must be done to determine whether I or that band of ruffians own those oyster beds."

"Now we'll see Neil," Charley said, when he had seen Mr. Taft upon his train to San Francisco.

Not only did Neil Partington interpose no obstacle to our adventure, but he proved to be of the greatest assistance. Charley and I knew nothing of the oyster industry, while his head was an encyclopedia of facts concerning it. Also, within an hour or so, he was able to bring to us a Greek boy of 17 or 18 who knew thoroughly well the ins and outs of oyster piracy.

At this point, I may as well explain that we of the fish patrol were freelancers in a way. While Neil Partington, who was a patrolman proper, received a regular salary, Charley and I, being merely deputies, received only what we earned—that is to say, a certain percentage of the fines imposed on convicted violators of the fish laws. Also, any rewards that chanced our way were ours. We offered to share with Partington whatever we should get from Mr. Taft, but the patrolman would not hear of it. He was only too happy, he said, to do a good turn for us, who had done so many for him.

We held a long council of war and mapped out the following line of action. Our faces were unfamiliar on the Lower Bay, but the *Reindeer* was well known as a fish-patrol sloop. The Greek boy, whose name was Nicholas, and I were to sail some innocent-looking craft down to Asparagus Island and join the oyster pirates' fleet. Here, according to Nicholas's description of the beds and the manner of raiding, it was possible for us to catch the pirates in the act of stealing oysters and at the same time to get them in our power. Charley was to be on the shore with Mr. Taft's watchmen and a posse of constables to help us at the right time.

"I know just the boat," Neil said, at the conclusion of the discussion "a crazy old sloop that's lying over at Tiburon. You and Nicholas can go over by the ferry, charter it for a song, and sail direct for the beds."

"Good luck be with you, boys," he said at parting, two days later. "Remember, they are dangerous men, so be careful."

Nicholas and I succeeded in chartering the sloop very cheaply; and between laughs, while getting up sail, we agreed that she was even crazier and older than she had been described. She was a big, flat-bottomed, square-sterned craft, sloop-rigged, with a sprung mast, slack rigging, dilapidated sails, and rotten running gear, clumsy to handle and uncertain in bringing about, and she smelled vilely of coal tar with which strange stuff she had been smeared from stem to stern and from cabin roof to centerboard. And to cap it all, *Coal Tar Maggie* was printed in great white letters the whole length of either side.

It was an uneventful though laughable run from Tiburon to Asparagus Island, where we arrived in the afternoon of the following day. The oyster pirates, a fleet of a dozen sloops, were lying at anchor on what was known as the "Deserted Beds." The *Coal Tar Maggie* came sloshing into their midst with a light breeze astern, and they crowded on deck to see us. Nicholas and I had caught the spirit of the crazy craft, and we handled her in most lubbery fashion.

"What is it?" someone called.

"Name it and ye can have it!" called another.

"I swear now, if it ain't the old Ark itself!" mimicked the Centipede from the deck of the *Ghost*.

"Hey! Ahoy there, clipper ship!" another wag shouted. "What's your port?"

We took no notice of the joking, but acted, after the manner of greenhorns, as though the *Coal Tar Maggie* required our undivided attention. I rounded her well to windward of the *Ghost*, and Nicholas ran forward to drop the anchor. To all appearances it was a bungle, the way the chain tangled and kept the anchor from reaching the bottom. And to all appearances Nicholas and I were terribly excited as we strove to clear it. At any rate, we quite deceived the pirates, who took huge delight in our predicament.

But the chain remained tangled, and amid all kinds of mocking advice we drifted down upon and fouled the *Ghost*, whose bowsprit poked square through our mainsail and ripped a hole in it as big as a barn door. The Centipede and the Porpoise doubled up on the cabin in paroxysms of laughter, and left us to get clear as best we could. This, with much unseamanlike performance, we succeeded in doing, and likewise in clearing the anchor chain, of which we let out about 300 feet. With only 10 feet of water under us, this would permit the *Coal Tar Maggie* to swing in a circle 600 feet in diameter, in which she would be able to foul at least half the fleet.

The oyster pirates lay snugly together at short hawsers, the weather being fine, and they protested loudly at our ignorance in putting out such an unwarranted length of anchor chain. And not only did they protest, for they made us heave it in again, all but 30 feet.

Having sufficiently impressed them with our general lubberliness, Nicholas and I went below to congratulate ourselves and to cook supper. Hardly had we finished the meal and washed the dishes when a skiff ground against the *Coal Tar Maggie's* side, and heavy feet trampled on deck. Then the Centipede's brutal face appeared in the companionway, and he descended into the cabin followed by the Porpoise. Before they could seat themselves on a bunk, another skiff came alongside, and another, and another, till the whole fleet was represented by the gathering in the cabin.

"Where'd you swipe the old tub?" asked a squat and hairy man, with cruel eyes.

"Didn't swipe it," Nicholas answered, meeting them on their own ground and encouraging the idea that we had stolen the *Coal Tar Maggie*. "And if we did, what of it?"

"Well, I don't admire your taste, that's all," sneered he. "I'd rot on the beach first before I'd take a tub that couldn't get out of its own way."

"How were we to know till we tried her?" Nicholas asked, so innocently as to cause a laugh. "And how do you get the oysters?" he hurried on. "We want a load of them. That's what we came for, a load of oysters."

"What d'you want 'em for?" demanded the Porpoise.

"Oh, to give away to our friends, of course," Nicholas retorted. "That's what you do with yours, I suppose."

This started another laugh, and as our visitors grew more genial we could see that they had not the slightest suspicion of our identity or purpose.

"Didn't I see you on the dock in Oakland the other day?" the Centipede asked suddenly of me.

"Yep," I answered boldly, taking the bull by the horns. "I was watching you fellows and figuring out whether we'd go oystering or not. It's a pretty good business, I calculate, and so we're going in for it. That is," I hastened to add, "if you fellows don't mind."

"I'll tell you one thing, which ain't two things," he replied, "and that is you'll have to hurry and get a better boat. We won't stand to be disgraced by any such box as this. Understand?"

"Sure," I said. "Soon as we well some oysters we'll outfit in style."

"And if you show yourself square and the right sort," he went on, "why, you can run with us. But if you don't" (here his voice became stern and menacing), "why, it'll be the sickest day of your life. Understand?"

"Sure," I said.

After that and more warning and advice of similar nature, the conversation became general, and we learned that the beds were to be raided that very night. As they got into their boats, after an hour's stay, we were invited to join them in the raid with the assurance of "the more the merrier."

"Did you notice that short, dark-haired chap?" Nicholas asked, when they had departed to their various sloops. "He's Barchi, of the Sporting Life Gang, and the fellow that came with him is Skilling. They're both out now on $5,000 bail."

I had heard of the Sporting Life Gang before, a crowd of hoodlums and criminals that terrorized the lower quarters of Oakland, and two-thirds of which were usually to be found in state's prison for crimes that ranged from perjury and ballot-box stuffing to murder.

"They are not regular oyster pirates," Nicholas continued. "They've just come down for the lark and to make a few dollars. But we'll have to watch out for them."

We sat in the cockpit and discussed the details of our plan till 11 o'clock had passed, when we heard the rattle of an oar in a boat from the direction of the *Ghost*. We hauled up our own skiff, tossed in a few sacks, and rowed over. There we found all the skiffs assembling, it being the intention to raid the beds as a group.

To my surprise, I found barely a foot of water where we had dropped anchor in 10 feet. It was the big June run-out of the full moon, and as the ebb had yet an hour and a half to run, I knew that our anchorage would be dry ground before slack water.

Mr. Taft's beds were three miles away, and for a long time we rowed silently in the wake of the other boats, once in a while grounding and our oar blades constantly striking bottom. At last we came upon soft mud covered with not more than two inches of water—not enough to float the boats. But the pirates at once were over the side, and by pushing and pulling on the flat-bottomed skiffs, we moved steadily along.

The full moon was partly obscured by high-flying clouds, but the pirates went their way with the familiarity born of long practice. After half a mile of the mud, we came upon a deep channel, up which we rowed, with dead oyster shoals looming high and dry on either side. At last we reached the picking grounds. Two men on one of the shoals hailed us and warned us off. But the Centipede, the Porpoise, Barchi, and Skilling took the lead, and followed by the rest of us, at least thirty men in half as many boats, rowed right up to the watchmen.

"You'd better slide outa this here," Barchi said threateningly, "or we'll fill you so full of holes you wouldn't float in molasses."

The watchmen wisely retreated before so overwhelming a force and rowed their boat along the channel toward where the shore should be. Besides, it was in the plan for them to retreat.

We hauled the noses of the boats up on the shore side of a big shoal and all hands with sacks spread out and began picking. Every now and again the clouds thinned before the face of the moon, and we could see the big oysters quite distinctly. In almost no time sacks were filled and carried back to the boats, where fresh ones were obtained. Nicholas and I returned often and anxiously to the boats with ourlittle loads but always found one of the pirates coming or going.

"Never mind," he said, "no hurry. As they pick farther and farther away, it will take too long to carry to the boats. Then they'll stand the full sacks on end and pick them up when the tide comes in and the skiffs will float to them."

Fully half an hour went by and the tide had begun to flood, when this came to pass. Leaving the pirates at their work, we stole back to the boats. One by one, and noiselessly, we shoved them off and made them fast in an awkward flotilla. Just as we were shoving off the last skiff, our own, one of the men came upon us. It was Barchi. His quick eye took in the situation at a glance, and he sprang for us. But we went clear with a mighty shove, and he was left floundering in the water over his head. As soon as he got back to the shoal he raised his voice and gave the alarm.

We rowed with all our strength, but it was slow going with so many boats in tow. A pistol cracked from the shoal, a second, and a third; then a regular fusillade began. The bullets spat and spat all about us; but thick clouds had covered the moon, and in the dim darkness it was no more than random firing. It was only by chance that we could be hit.

"Wish we had a little steam launch," I panted.

"I'd just as soon the moon stayed hidden," Nicholas panted back.

It was slow work, but every stroke carried us farther away from the shoal and nearer the shore, till at last the shooting died down, and when the moon did come out we were too far away to be in danger. Not long afterward we answered a shoreward hail, and two Whitehall boats, each pulled by three pairs of oars, darted up to us. Charley's welcome face bent over to us, and he gripped us by the hands while he cried, "Oh, you joys! You joys! Both of you!"

When the flotilla had been landed, Nicholas and I, and a watchman rowed out in one of the Whitehalls with Charley in the stern sheets. Two other Whitehalls followed us, and as the moon now shone brightly, we easily made out the oyster pirates on their lonely shoal. As we drew closer they fired a rattling volley from their revolvers, and we promptly retreated beyond range.

"Lot of time," Charley said. "The flood is setting in fast, and by the time it's up to their necks there won't be any fight left in them."

So we lay on our oars and waited for the tide to do its work. This was the predicament of the pirates: because of the big run-out, the tide was now rushing back like a millrace, and it was impossible for the strongest swimmer in the world to make against it the three miles to the sloops. Between the pirates and the shore were we, precluding escape in that direction. On the other hand, the water was rising rapidly over the shoals, and it was only a question of a few hours when it would be over their heads.

It was beautifully calm, and in the brilliant white moonlight we watched them through our night glasses and told Charley of the voyage of the *Coal Tar Maggie*. One o'clock came, and two o'clock, and the pirates were clustering on the highest shoal, waist-deep in water.

"Now this illustrates the value of imagination," Charley was saying. "Taft has been trying for years to get them, but he went at it with bull strength and failed. Now we used our heads. . . ."

Just then I heard a scarcely audible gurgle of water, and holding up my hand for silence, I turned and pointed to a ripple slowly widening out in a growing circle. It was not more than 50 feet from us. We kept perfectly quiet and waited. After a minute the water broke six feet away, and a black head and white shoulder showed in the moonlight. With a snort of surprise and of suddenly expelled breath, the head and shoulder went down.

We pulled ahead several strokes and drifted with the current. Four pairs of eyes searched the surface of the water, but never another ripple showed, and never another glimpse did we catch of the black head and white shoulder.

"It's the Porpoise," Nicholas said. "It would take broad daylight for us to catch him."

At a quarter to three the pirates gave their first sign of weakening. We heard cries for help, in the unmistakable voice of the Centipede, and this time, on rowing closer, we were not fired upon. The Centipede was in a truly perilous plight. Only the heads and shoulders of his fellow marauders showed above the water as they braced themselves against the current, while his feet were off the bottom and they were supporting him.

"Now, lads," Charley said briskly, "we have got you, and you can't get away. If you cut up rough, we'll have to leave you alone and the water will finish you. But if you're good we'll take you aboard, one man at a time, and you'll all be saved. What do you say?"

"Ay," they chorused hoarsely between their chattering teeth.

"Then one man at a time, and the short men first."

The Centipede was the first to be pulled aboard, and he came willingly, though he objected when the constable put the handcuffs on him. Barchi was next hauled in, quite meek and resigned from his soaking. When we had ten in, our boat drew back, and the second Whitehall was loaded. The third Whitehall received nine prisoners only—a catch of 29 in all.

"You didn't get the Porpoise," the Centipede said exultantly, as though his escape materially diminished our success.

Charley laughed. "But we saw him just the same, a-snorting for shore like a puffing pig."

It was a mild and shivering band of pirates that we marched up the beach to the oyster house. In answer to Charley's knock, the door was flung open, and a pleasant wave of warm air rushed out upon us.

"You can dry your clothes here, lads, and get some hot coffee," Charley announced, as they filed in.

And there, sitting ruefully by the fire, with a steaming mug in his hand, was the Porpoise. With one accord Nicholas and I looked at Charley. He laughed gleefully.

"That comes of imagination," he said. "When you see a thing, you've got to see it all around, or what's the good of seeing it at all? I saw the beach, so I left a couple of constables behind to keep an eye on it. That's all."

AT THE EDGE OF THE CRATER

FROM THE BROTHERHOOD OF THE SEVEN KINGS

L. T. Meade
(1854–1914)
and
Robert Eustace
(1854–1947?)

L. T. (ELIZABETH THOMASINA) MEADE was the daughter of a rector, or pastor, in County Cork, Ireland. She wrote her first book at age 17 and many more followed. In fact, Meade wrote more than 250 books and stories—especially during the 1890s and in the early years of the twentieth century. She most often penned stories about girls at school, but she also wrote a great many detective stories and adventures, like this one. Meade, with her partner Eustace, created one of the first female detectives, a character called Florence Cusack. Although such characters were quite unusual at the time, the pair also introduced two frightening female villains, one of whom makes a brief, but important, appearance in this tale. Among Meade's many other exciting stories are "The Sorceress of the Strand," "House of Black

Magic," "The Sanctuary Club," "The Brotherhood of the Seven Kings," and "The Man Who Disappeared." A few of her popular stories for girls include "Priscilla's Promise," "Sweet Girl Graduate," and "The Time of Roses."

Robert Eustace is the *nom de plume*, or penname, for Dr. Eustace Robert Barton. Not much is known about Eustace, although he worked with a number of other authors and helped to produce hundreds of stories and several novels. In addition to the exciting adventures he wrote with Meade, Eustace also collaborated with Edgar Jepson and Dorothy Sayers. By 1947 Dr. Barton was retired and said to be "traveling." No record of his death has been found in any medical publication.

INTRODUCTION

That a secret society, based upon the lines of similar institutions so notorious on the Continent during the last century, could ever have existed in the London of our day may seem impossible. Such a society, however, not only did exist, but through the instrumentality of a woman of unparalleled capacity and genius, obtained a firm footing. A century ago the Brotherhood of the Seven Kings was a name hardly whispered without horror and fear in Italy, and now, by the fascinations and influence of one woman, it began to accomplish fresh deeds of unparalleled daring and subtlety in London. By the wide extent of its scientific resources, and the impregnable secrecy of its organizations, it threatened to become a formidable menace to society, as well as a source of serious anxiety to the authorities of the law. It is to the courtesy of Mr. Norman Head that we are indebted for the subject-matter of the following hitherto unpublished revelations.

TOLD BY NORMAN HEAD

It was in the year 1894 that the first of the remarkable events which I am about to give to the world occurred. They found me something of a philosopher and a recluse, having, as I thought, lived my life and done with the active part of existence. It is true that I was young, not more than 35 years of age, but in the ghastly past I had committed a supreme error, and because of that paralyzing experience I had left the bustling world and found my solace in the scientist's laboratory and the philosopher's study.

Ten years before these stories begin, when in Naples studying biology, I fell victim to the wiles and fascinations of a beautiful Italian. A scientist of no mean attainments herself, with beauty beyond that of ordinary mortals, she had appealed not only to my head, but also to my heart. Dazzled by her beauty and intellect, she led me where she would. Her aims and ambitions, which in the false glamour she threw over them I thought the loftiest in the world, became also mine. She introduced me to the men of her set—I was quickly in the toils, and on a night never to be forgotten, I took part in a grotesque and horrible ceremony, and became a member of her Brotherhood.

It was called the Brotherhood of the Seven Kings, and dated its origin from one of the secret societies of the Middle

Ages. In my first enthusiasm it seemed to me to embrace all the principles of true liberty. Katherine was its chief and queen. Almost immediately after my initiation, however, I made an appalling discovery. Suspicion pointed to the beautiful Italian as the instigator, if not the author, of a most terrible crime. None of the details could be brought home to her, but there was little doubt that she was its moving spring. Loving her passionately as I then did, I tried to close my intellect against the all too conclusive evidence of her guilt. For a time I succeeded, but when I was ordered myself to take part in a transaction both dishonorable and treacherous, my eyes were opened. Horror seized me, and I fled to England to place myself under the protection of its laws.

Ten years went by, and the past was beginning to fade. It was destined to be recalled to me with startling vividness.

When a young man at Cambridge I had studied physiology, but never qualified myself as a doctor, having independent means; but in my laboratory in the vicinity of Regent's Park I worked at biology and physiology for the pure love of these absorbing sciences.

I was busily engaged on the afternoon of the 3rd of August, 1894, when Mrs. Kenyon, an old friend, called to see me. She was shown into my study, and I went to her there. Mrs. Kenyon was a widow, but her son, a lad of about 12 years of age, had, owing to the unexpected death of a relative, just come in for a large fortune and a title. She took the seat I offered her.

"It is too bad of you, Norman," she said; "it is months since you have been near me. Do you intend to forget your old friends?"

"I hope you will forgive me," I answered; "you know how busy I always am."

"You work too hard," she replied. "Why a man with your brains and opportunities for enjoying life wishes to shut himself up in the way you do, I cannot imagine."

"I am quite happy as I am, Mrs. Kenyon," I replied; "why, therefore, should I change? By the way, how is Cecil?"

"I have come here to speak about him. You know, of course, the wonderful change in his fortunes?"

"Yes," I answered.

"He has succeeded to the Kairn property, and is now Lord Kairn. There is a large rent-roll and considerable estates. You know, Norman, that Cecil has always been a most delicate boy."

"I hoped you were about to tell me that he was stronger," I replied.

"He is, and I will explain how in a moment. His life is a most important one. As Lord Kairn much is expected of him. He has not only, under the providence of God, to live, but by that one little life he has to keep a man of exceedingly bad character out of a great property. I allude to Hugh Doncaster. Were Cecil to die, Hugh would be Lord Kairn. You have already doubtless heard of his character?"

"I know the man well by repute," I said.

"I thought you did. His disappointment and rage at Cecil succeeding to the title are almost beyond bounds. Rumors of his malevolent feelings toward the child have already reached me. I am told that he is now in London, but his life, like yours, is more or less mysterious. I thought it just possible, Norman,

177

that you, as an old friend, might be able to get me some particulars with regard to his whereabouts."

"Why do you want to know?" I asked.

"I feel a strange uneasiness about him; something which I cannot account for. Of course, in these enlightened days he would not attempt the child's life, but I should be more comfortable if I were assured that he were nowhere in Cecil's vicinity."

"But the man can do nothing to your boy!" I said. "Of course, I will find out what I can, but—"

Mrs. Kenyon interrupted me.

"Thank you. It is a relief to know that you will help me. Of course, there is no real danger; but I am a widow, and Cecil is only a child. Now, I must tell you about his health. He is almost quite well. The most marvelous resurrection has taken place. For the last two months he has been under the care of that extraordinary woman, Mme. Koluchy. She has worked miracles in his case, and now to complete the cure she is sending him to the Mediterranean. He sails tomorrow night under the care of Dr. Fietta. I cannot bear parting with him, but it is for his good, and Mme. Koluchy insists that a sea voyage is indispensable."

"But won't you accompany him?" I asked.

"I am sorry to say that is impossible. My eldest girl, Ethel, is about to be married, and I cannot leave her on the eve of her wedding; but Cecil will be in good hands. Dr. Fietta is a capital fellow—I have every faith in him."

"Where are they going?"

"To Cairo. They sail tomorrow night in the Hydaspes."

"Cairo is a fearfully hot place at this time of year. Are you quite sure that it is wise to send a delicate lad like Cecil there in August?"

"Oh, he will not stay. He sails for the sake of the voyage, and will come back by the return boat. The voyage is, according to Mme. Koluchy, to complete the cure. That marvelous woman has succeeded where the medical profession gave little hope. You have heard of her, of course?"

"I am sick of her very name," I replied; "one hears it everywhere. She has bewitched London with her impostures and quackery."

"There is no quackery about her, Norman. I believe her to be the cleverest woman in England. There are authentic accounts of her wonderful cures which cannot be contradicted. There are even rumors that she is able to restore youth and beauty by her arts. The whole of society is at her feet, and it is whispered that even royalty are among her patients. Of course, her fees are enormous, but look at the results! Have you ever met her?"

"Never. Where does she come from? Who is she?"

"She is an Italian, but she speaks English perfectly. She has taken a house which is a perfect palace in Welbeck Street."

"And who is Dr. Fietta?"

"A medical man who assists Madame in her treatments. I have just seen him. He is charming, and devoted to Cecil. Five o'clock! I had no idea it was so late. I must be going. You will let me know when you hear any news of Mr. Doncaster? Come and see me soon."

I accompanied my visitor to the door, and then, returning

to my study, sat down to resume the work I had been engaged in when I was interrupted.

But Mrs. Kenyon's visit had made me restless. I knew Hugh Doncaster's character well. Reports of his evil ways now and then agitated society, but the man had hitherto escaped the stern arm of justice. Of course, there could be no real foundation for Mrs. Kenyon's fears, but I felt that I could sympathize with her. The child was young and delicate; if Doncaster could injure him without discovery, he would not scruple to do so. As I thought over these things, a vague sensation of coming trouble possessed me. I hastily got into my evening dress, and having dined at my club, found myself at half-past 10 in a drawing-room in Grosvenor Square. As I passed on into the reception-rooms, having exchanged a few words with my hostess, I came across Dufrayer, a lawyer, and a special friend of mine. We got into conversation. As we talked, and my eyes glanced idly round the groups of smartly dressed people, I noticed where a crowd of men were clustering round and paying homage to a stately woman at the farther end of the room. A diamond star flashed in her dusky hair. On her neck and arms diamonds also glittered. She had an upright bearing and a regal appearance. Her rosy lips were smiling. The marked intelligence and power of her face could not fail to arrest attention, even in the most casual observer. At the first glance I felt that I had seen her before, but could not tell when or where.

"Who is that woman?" I asked of my companion.

"My dear fellow," he replied, with an amused smile, "don't you know? That is the great Mme. Koluchy, the rage of the season, the great specialist, the great consultant. London is mad about her. She has only been here 10 minutes, and look, she is going already. They say she has a dozen engagements every night."

Mme. Koluchy began to move toward the door, and, anxious to get a nearer view, I also passed rapidly through the throng. I reached the head of the stairs before she did, and as she went by looked her full in the face. Her eyes met mine. Their dark depths seemed to read me through. She half smiled, half paused as if to speak, changed her mind, made a stately inclination of her queenly head, and went slowly downstairs. For a moment I stood still, there was a ringing in my ears, and my heart was beating to suffocation. Then I hastily followed her. When I reached the pavement Mme. Koluchy's carriage stopped the way. She did not notice me, but I was able to observe her. She was bending out and talking eagerly to some one. The following words fell on my ear:

"It is all right. They sail tomorrow evening."

The man to whom she spoke made a reply which I could not catch, but I had seen his face. He was Hugh Doncaster.

Mme. Koluchy's carriage rolled away, and I hailed a hansom. In supreme moments we think rapidly. I thought quickly then.

"Where to?" asked the driver.

"No. 140, Earl's Terrace, Kensington," I called out. I sat back as I spoke. The horror of past memories was almost paralyzing me, but I quickly pulled myself together. I knew that I must act, and act quickly. I had just seen the Head of the Brotherhood of the Seven Kings. Mme. Koluchy, changed in

181

much since I last saw her, was the woman who had wrecked my heart and life 10 years ago in Naples.

With my knowledge of the past, I was well aware that where this woman appeared victims fell. Her present victim was a child. I must save that child, even if my own life were the penalty. She had ordered the boy abroad. He was to sail tomorrow with an emissary of hers. She was in league with Doncaster. If she could get rid of the boy, Doncaster would doubtless pay her a fabulous sum. For the working of her she above all things wanted money. Yes, without doubt the lad's life was in the gravest danger, and I had not a moment to lose. The first thing was to communicate with the mother, and if possible put a stop to the intended voyage.

I arrived at the house, flung open the doors of the hansom, and ran up the steps. Here unexpected news awaited me. The servant who answered my summons said that Mrs. Kenyon had started for Scotland by the night mail—she had received a telegram announcing the serious illness of her eldest girl. On getting it she had started for the north, but would not reach her destination until the following evening.

"Is Lord Kairn in?" I asked.

"No, sir," was the reply. "My mistress did not like to leave him here alone, and he has been sent over to Mme. Koluchy's, 100 Welbeck Street. Perhaps you are not aware, sir, that his lordship sails tomorrow evening for Cairo?"

"Yes, I know all about that," I replied "and now, if you will give me your mistress's address, I shall be much obliged to you."

The man supplied it. I entered my hansom again. For a moment it occurred to me that I would send a telegram to intercept Mrs. Kenyon on her rapid journey north, but I finally made up my mind not to do so. The boy was already in the enemy's hands, and I felt sure that I could now only rescue him by guile. I returned home, having already made up my mind how to act. I would accompany Cecil and Dr. Fietta to Cairo.

At 11 o'clock on the following morning I had taken my berth in the Hydaspes, and at nine that evening was on board. I caught a momentary glimpse of young Lord Kairn and his attendant, but in order to avoid explanations kept out of their way. It was not until the following morning, when the steamer was well down the channel, that I made my appearance on deck, where I at once saw the boy sitting at the stern in a chair. Beside him was a lean, middle-aged man wearing a pair of pince-nez. He looked every inch a foreigner, with his pointed beard, waxed moustache, and deep-set, beady eyes. As I sauntered across the deck to where they were sitting, Lord Kairn looked up and instantly recognized me.

"Mr. Head!" he exclaimed, jumping from his chair, "you here? I am very glad to see you."

"I am on my way to Cairo, on business," I said, shaking the boy warmly by the hand.

"To Cairo? Why, that is where we are going; but you never told mother you were coming, and she saw you the day before yesterday. It was such a pity that mother had to rush off to Scotland so suddenly; but last night, just before we sailed, there came a telegram telling us that Ethel was better. As mother had to go away, I went to Mme. Koluchy's for the night. I love going there. She has a lovely house, and she is so delightful herself. And this is Dr. Fietta, who has come with me." As the boy added these words Dr. Fietta came forward and peered at me through his pince-nez. I bowed, and he returned my salutation.

"This is an extraordinary coincidence, Dr. Fietta!" I exclaimed. "Cecil Kenyon happens to be the son of one of my greatest friends. I am glad to see him looking so well. Whatever Mme. Koluchy's treatment has been, it has had a marvelous effect. I am told that you are fortunate enough to be the participator in her wonderful secrets and cures."

"I have the honor of assisting Mme. Koluchy," he replied, with a strong foreign accent; "but may I take the liberty of inquiring who gave you the information about myself?"

"It was Mrs. Kenyon," I answered. "She told me all about you the other day."

"She knew, then, that you were going to be a fellow-passenger of her son's?"

"No, for I did not know myself. An urgent telegram calling me to Egypt arrived that evening, and I only booked my passage yesterday. I am fortunate in having the honor of meeting so distinguished a savant as yourself. I have heard much about Mme. Koluchy's marvelous occult powers, but I suppose the secrets of her success are very jealously guarded. The profession, of course, pooh-pooh her, I know, but if one may credit all one hears, she possesses remedies undreamt-of in their philosophy."

"It is quite true, Mr. Head. As a medical man myself, I can vouch for her capacity, and, unfettered by English professional scrupulousness, I appreciate it. Mme. Koluchy and I are proud of our young friend here, and hope that the voyage will complete his cure, and fit him for the high position he is destined to occupy."

The voyage flew by. Fietta was an intelligent man, and his scientific attainments were considerable. But for my knowledge of the terrible past my fears might have slumbered, but as it was they were always present with me, and the moment all too quickly arrived when suspicion was to be plunged into certainty.

On the day before we were due at Malta, the wind sprang up and we got into a choppy sea. When I had finished breakfast I went to Cecil's cabin to see how he was. He was just getting up, and looked pale and unwell.

"There is a nasty sea on," I said, "but the captain says we shall be out of it in an hour or so."

"I hope we shall," he answered, "for it makes me feel squeamish, but I daresay I shall be all right when I get on deck. Dr. Fietta has given me something to stop the sickness, but it has not had much effect."

"I do not know anything that really stops sea-sickness," I answered; "but what has he done?"

"Oh: a curious thing, Mr. Head. He pricked my arm with a needle on a syringe, and squirted something in. He says it is a certain cure for sea-sickness. Look," said the child, baring his arm, "that is where he did it."

I examined the mark closely. It had evidently been made with a hypodermic injection needle.

"Did Dr. Fietta tell you what he put into your arm?" I asked.

"Yes, he said it was morphia."

"Where does he keep his needle?"

"In his trunk there under his bunk. I shall be dressed directly, and will come on deck."

I left the cabin and went up the companion. The doctor was pacing to and fro on the hurricane-deck. I approached him.

"Your charge has not been well," I said. "I have just seen him. He tells me you have give him a hypodermic of morphia."

He turned round and gave me a quick glance of uneasy fear.

"Did Lord Kairn tell you so?"

"Yes."

"Well, Mr. Head, it is the very best cure for sea-sickness. I have found it most efficacious."

"Do you think it wise to give a child morphia?" I asked.

"I do not discuss my treatment with an unqualified man," he replied brusquely, turning away as he spoke. I looked after him, and as he disappeared down the deck my fears became certainties. I determined, come what would, to find out what he had given the boy. I knew only too well the infinite possibilities of that dangerous little instrument, a hypodermic syringe.

As the day wore on the sea moderated, and at five o'clock it was quite calm again, a welcome change to the passengers, who, with the permission of the captain, had arranged to give a dance that evening on deck. The occasion was one when ordinary scruples must fade out of sight. Honor in such a mission, as I had set myself must give place to the watchful zeal of the detective. I was determined to take advantage of the dance to explore Dr. Fietta's cabin. The doctor was fond of dancing, and as soon as I saw that he and Lord Kairn were well engaged, I descended the companion, and went to their cabin. I switched on the electric light, and, dragging the trunk from beneath the bunk, hastily opened it. It was unlocked and only secured by straps. I ran my hand rapidly through the contents, which were chiefly clothes, but tucked in one corner I found a case, and, pulling it out, opened it. Inside lay the delicate little hypodermic syringe which I had come in search of.

I hurried up to the light and examined it. Smeared round the inside of the glass, and adhering to the bottom of the little plunger, was a whitish, gelatinous-looking substance. This was no ordinary hypodermic solution. It was half-liquefied gelatin such as I knew so well as the medium for the cultivation of micro-organisms. For a moment I felt half-stunned. What infernal culture might it not contain?

Time was flying, and at any moment I might be discovered. I hastily slipped the syringe into my pocket, and closing the trunk, replaced it, and, switching off the electric light, returned to the deck. My temples were throbbing, and it was with difficulty I could keep my self-control. I made up my mind quickly. Fietta would of course miss the syringe, but the chances were that he would not do so that night. As yet there was nothing apparently the matter with the boy, but might there not be flowing through his veins some poisonous germs of disease, which only required a period of incubation for their development?

At daybreak the boat would arrive at Malta. I would go on shore at once, call upon some medical man, and lay the case before him in confidence, in the hope of his having the things

I should need in order to examine the contents of the syringe. If I found any organisms, I would take the law into my own hands, and carry the boy back to England by the next boat.

No sleep visited me that night, and I lay tossing to and fro in my bunk longing for daylight. At six o'clock. I heard the engine-bell ring, and the screw suddenly slow down to half-speed. I leapt up and went on deck. I could see the outline of the rock-bound fortress and the lighthouse of St. Elmo looming more vividly every moment. As soon as we were at anchor and the gangway down, I hailed one of the little green boats and told the men to row me to the shore. I drove at once to the Grand Hotel in the Strada Reale, and asked the Italian guide the address of a medical man. He gave me the address of an English doctor who lived close by, and I went there at once to see him. It was now seven o'clock, and I found him up. I made my apologies for the early hour of my visit, put the whole matter before him, and produced the syringe. For a moment he was inclined to take my story with incredulity, but by degrees he became interested, and ended by inviting me to breakfast with him. After the meal we repaired to his consulting-room to make our investigations. He brought out his microscope, which I saw, to my delight, was of the latest design, and I set to work at once, while he watched me with evident interest. At last the crucial moment came, and I bent over the instrument and adjusted the focus on my preparation. My suspicions were only too well confirmed by which I had extracted what I saw. The substance from the syringe was a mass of micro-organisms, but of what nature I did not know. I had never seen any quite like them before. I drew back.

"I wish you would look at this," I said. "You tell me you have devoted considerable attention to bacteriology. Please tell me what you see."

Dr. Benson applied his eye to the instrument, regulating the focus for a few moments in silence, then he raised his head, and looked at me with a curious expression.

"Where did this culture come from?" he asked.

"From London, I presume," I answered.

"It is extraordinary," he said, with emphasis, "but there is no doubt whatever that these organisms are the specific germs of the very disease I have studied here so assiduously; they are the micrococci of Mediterranean fever, the minute round or oval bacteria. They are absolutely characteristic."

I jumped to my feet.

"Is that so?" I cried. The diabolical nature of the plot was only too plain. These germs injected into a patient would produce a fever which only occurs in the Mediterranean. The fact that the boy had been in the Mediterranean even for a short time would be a complete blind as to the way in which they obtained access to the body, as every one would think the disease occurred from natural causes.

"How long is the period of incubation?" I asked.

"About 10 days," replied Dr. Benson.

I extended my hand.

"You have done me an invaluable service," I said.

"I may possibly be able to do you a still further service," was his reply. "I have made Mediterranean fever the study of my life, and have, I believe, discovered an antitoxin for it. I have tried my discovery on the patients of the naval hospital with excellent results. The local disturbance is slight, and I have never found bad symptoms follow the treatment. If you will bring the boy to me I will administer the antidote without delay."

I considered for a moment, then I said: "My position is a terrible one, and I am inclined to accept your proposition. Under the circumstances it is the only chance."

"It is," repeated Dr. Benson. "I shall be at your service whenever you need me."

I bade him good-bye and quickly left the house.

It was now 10 o'clock. My first object was to find Dr. Fietta, to speak to him boldly, and take the boy away by main force if necessary. I rushed back to the Grand Hotel, where I learned that a boy and a man, answering to the description of Dr. Fietta and Cecil, had breakfasted there, but had gone out again immediately afterward. The Hydaspes I knew was to coal, and would not leave Malta before one o'clock. My only chance, therefore, was to catch them as they came on board. Until then I could do nothing. At 12 o'clock I went down to the quay and took a boat to the Hydaspes. Seeing no sign of Fietta and the boy on deck, I made my way at once to Lord Kairn's cabin. The door was open and the place in confusion— every vestige of baggage had disappeared. Absolutely at a loss to divine the cause of this unexpected discovery, I pressed the electric bell. In a moment a steward appeared.

"Has Lord Kairn left the ship?" I asked, my heart beating fast.

"I believe so, sir," replied the man. "I had orders to pack the luggage and send it on shore. It went about an hour ago."

I waited to hear no more. Rushing to my cabin, I began flinging my things pell-mell into my portmanteau. I was full of apprehension at this sudden move of Dr. Fietta's. Calling a steward who was passing to help me, I got my things on deck, and in a few moments had them in a boat and was making rapidly for the shore. I drove back at once to the Grand Hotel in the Strada Reale.

"Did the gentleman who came here today from the Hydaspes, accompanied by a little boy, engage rooms for the night?" I asked of the proprietor in the bureau at the top of the stairs.

"No, sir," answered the man; "they breakfasted here, but did not return. I think they said they were going to the gardens of San Antonio."

For a minute or two I paced the hall in uncontrollable excitement. I was completely at a loss what step to take next. Then suddenly an idea struck me. I hurried down the steps and made my way to Cook's office.

"A gentleman of that description took two tickets for Naples by the *Spartivento,* a Rupertino boat, two hours ago," said the clerk, in answer to my inquiries. "She has started by now," he continued, glancing up at the clock.

"To Naples?" I cried. A sickening fear seized me. The very name of the hated place struck me like a poisoned weapon.

"Is it too late to catch her?" I cried.

"Yes, sir, she has gone."

"Then what is the quickest route by which I can reach Naples?"

"You can go by the Gingra, a P. & O. boat, tonight to Brindisi, and then overland. That is the quickest way now."

I at once took my passage and left the office. There was

not the least doubt what had occurred. Dr. Fietta had missed his syringe, and in consequence had immediately altered his plans. He was now taking the lad to the very fountain-head of the Brotherhood, where other means if necessary would be employed to put an end to his life.

It was nine o'clock in the evening, three days later, when, from the window of the railway carriage, I caught my first glimpse of the glow on the summit of Vesuvius. During the journey I had decided on my line of action. Leaving my luggage in the cloak-room I entered a carriage and began to visit hotel after hotel. For a long time I had no success. It was past 11 o'clock that night when, weary and heart-sick, I drew up at the Hotel Londres. I went to the concierge with my usual question, expecting the invariable reply, but a glow of relief swept over me when the man said:

"Dr. Fietta is out, sir, but the young man is in. He is in bed—will you call tomorrow? What name shall I say?"

"I shall stay here," I answered. "Let me have a room at once, and have my bag taken to it. What is the number of Lord Kairn's room?"

"Number 46. But he will be asleep, sir; you cannot see him right now."

I made no answer, but going quickly upstairs, I found the boy's room. I knocked; there was no reply, I turned the handle and entered. All was dark. Striking a match I looked round. In a white bed at the farther end lay the child. I went up and bent softly over him. He was lying with one hand beneath his cheek. He looked worn and tired, and now and then moaned as if in trouble. When I touched him lightly on the shoulder he started up and opened his eyes. A dazed expression of surprise swept over his face; then with an eager cry he stretched out both his hands and clasped one of mine.

"I am so glad to see you," he said. "Dr. Fietta told me you were angry—that I had offended you. I very nearly cried when I missed you that morning at Malta, and Dr. Fietta said I should never see you any more. I don't like him—I am afraid of him. Have you come to take me home?" As he spoke he glanced eagerly round in the direction of the door, clutching my hand still tighter as he did so.

"Yes, I shall take you home, Cecil. I have come for the purpose," I answered; "but are you quite well?"

"That's just it; I am not. I have awful dreams at night. Oh, I am so glad you have come back and you are not angry. Did you say you were really going to take me home?"

"Tomorrow, if you like."

"Please do. I am—stoop down, I want to whisper to you—I am dreadfully afraid of Dr. Fietta."

"What is your reason?" I asked.

"There is no reason," answered the child, "but somehow I dread him. I have done so ever since you left us at Malta. Once I woke in the middle of the night and he was bending over me—he had such a queer look on his face, and he used that syringe again. He was putting something into my arm—he told me it was morphia. I did not want him to do it, for I thought you would rather he didn't. I wish mother had sent me away with you. I am afraid of him; yes, I am afraid of him."

"Now that I have come, everything will be right," I said.

"And you will take me home tomorrow?"

"Certainly."

"But I should like to see Vesuvius first. Now that we are here it seems a pity that I should not see it. Can you take me to Vesuvius tomorrow morning, and home in the evening, and will you explain to Dr. Fietta?"

"I will explain everything. Now go to sleep. I am in the house, and you have nothing whatever to fear."

"I am very glad you have come," he said wearily. He flung himself back on his pillow; the exhausted look was very manifest on his small, childish face. I left the room, shutting the door softly.

To say that my blood boiled can express but little the emotions which ran through my frame—the child was in the hands of a monster. He was in the very clutch of the Brotherhood, whose intention was to destroy his life. I thought for a moment. There was nothing now for it but to see Fietta, tell him that I had discovered his machinations, claim the boy, and take him away by force. I knew that I was treading on dangerous ground. At any moment my own life might be the forfeit for my supposed treachery to the cause whose vows I had so madly taken. Still, if I saved the boy nothing else really mattered.

I went downstairs into the great central hall, interviewed the concierge who told me that Fietta had returned, asked for the number of his private sitting-room, and, going there, opened the door without knocking. At a writing-table at the farther end sat the doctor. He turned as I entered, and, recognizing me, started up with a sudden exclamation. I noticed that his face changed color, and that his beady eyes flashed all ugly fire. Then, recovering himself, he advanced quietly toward me.

"This is another of your unexpected surprises, Mr. Head," he said with politeness. "You have not, then, gone on to Cairo? You change your plans rapidly."

"Not more so than you do, Dr. Fietta," I replied, watching him as I spoke.

"I was obliged to change my mind," he answered. "I heard in Malta that cholera had broken out in Cairo. I could not therefore take my patient there. May I inquire why I have the honor of this visit? You will excuse my saying so, but this action of yours forces me to suspect that you are following me. Have you a reason?"

He stood with his hands behind him, and a look of furtive vigilance crept into his small eyes.

"This is my reason," I replied. I boldly drew the hypodermic syringe from my pocket as I spoke.

With an inconceivably rapid movement he hurried past me, locked the door, and placed the key in his pocket. As he turned toward me again I saw the glint of a long, bright stiletto which he had drawn and was holding in his right hand, which he kept behind him.

"I see you are armed," I said quietly, "but do not be too hasty. I have a few words to say to you." As I spoke I looked him full in the face, then I dropped my voice.

"I am one of the Brotherhood of the Seven Kings!"

When I uttered these magical words he started back and looked at me with dilated eyes.

"Your proofs instantly, or you are a dead man," he cried hoarsely. Beads of sweat gleamed upon his forehead.

"Put that weapon on the table, give me your right hand, and you shall have the proofs you need," I answered.

195

He hesitated, then changed the stiletto to his left hand, and gave me his right. I grasped it in the peculiar manner which I had never forgotten, and bent my head close to his. The next moment I had uttered the password of the Brotherhood.

"La regina," I whispered.

"E la regina," he replied, flinging the stiletto on the carpet.

"Ah!" he continued, with an expression of the strongest relief, while he wiped the moisture from his forehead. "This is too wonderful. And now tell me, my friend, what your mission is? I knew you had stolen my syringe, but why did you do it? Why did you not reveal yourself to me before? You are, of course, under the Queen's orders?"

"I am," I answered, "and her orders to me now are to take Lord Kairn home to England overland tomorrow morning."

"Very well. Everything is finished—he will die in one month."

"From Mediterranean fever? But it is not necessarily fatal," I continued.

"That is true. It is not always fatal acquired in the ordinary way, but by our methods it is so."

"Then you have administered more of the micro-organisms since Malta?"

"Yes; I had another syringe in my case, and now nothing can save him. The fever will commence in six days from now."

He paused for a moment or two.

"It is very odd," he went on, "that I should have had no communication. I cannot understand it." A sudden flash of suspicion shot across his dark face. My heart sank as I saw it. It passed, however, the next instant; the man's words were courteous and quiet.

"I of course accede to your proposition," he said. "Everything is quite safe. This that I have done can never by any possibility be discovered. Madame is invincible. Have you yet seen Lord Kairn?"

"Yes, and I have told him to be prepared to accompany me home tomorrow."

"Very well."

Dr. Fietta walked across the room, unlocked the door and threw it open.

"Your plans will suit me admirably," he continued. "I shall stay on here for a few days more, as I have some private business to transact. Tonight I shall sleep in peace. Your shadow has been haunting me for the last three days.

I went from Fietta's room to the boy's. He was wide awake and started up when he saw me.

"I have arranged everything, Cecil," I said, "and you are my charge now. I mean to take you to my room to sleep."

"Oh," he answered, "I am glad. Perhaps I shall sleep better in your room. I am not afraid of you—I love you." His eyes, bright with affection, looked into mine. I lifted him into my arms, wrapped his dressing-gown over his shoulders, and conveyed him through the folding-doors, down the corridor, into the room I had secured for myself. There were two beds in the room, and I placed him in one.

"I am so happy," he said, "I love you so much. Will you take me to Vesuvius in the morning, and then home in the evening?"

"I will see about that. Now go to sleep," I answered.

He closed his eyes with a sigh of pleasure. In 10 minutes he was sound asleep. I was standing by him when there came a knock at the door. I went to open it. A waiter stood without. He held a salver in his hand. It contained a letter, also a sheet of paper and an envelope stamped with the name of the hotel.

"From the doctor, to be delivered to the signor immediately," was the laconic remark.

Still standing in the doorway, I took the letter from the tray, opened it, and read the following words:

"You have removed the boy and that action arouses my mistrust. I doubt your having received any communication from Madame. If you wish me to believe that you are a bona-fide member of the Brotherhood, return the boy to his own sleeping-room, immediately."

I took a pencil out of my pocket and hastily wrote a few words on the sheet of paper, which had been sent for this purpose.

"I retain the boy. You are welcome to draw your own conclusions."

Folding up the paper I slipped it into the envelope, and wetting the gum with my tongue, fastened it together, and handed it to the waiter who withdrew. I re-entered my room and locked the door. To keep the boy was imperative, but there was little doubt that Fietta would now telegraph to Mme. Koluchy (the telegraphic office being open day and night) and find out the trick I was playing upon him. I considered whether I might not remove the boy there and then to another hotel, but decided that such a step would be useless. Once the emissaries of the Brotherhood were put upon my track the case for the child and myself would be all but hopeless.

There was likely to be little sleep for me that night. I paced up and down my lofty room. My thoughts were keen and busy. After a time, however, a strange confusion seized me. One moment I thought of the child, the next of Mme. Koluchy, and then again I found myself pondering some abstruse and comparatively unimportant point in science, which I was perfecting at home. I shook myself free of these thoughts, to walk about again, to pause by the bedside of the child, to listen to his quiet breathing.

Perfect peace reigned over his little face. He had resigned himself to me, his terrors were things of the past, and he was absolutely happy. Then once again that odd confusion of brain returned. I wondered what I was doing, and why I was anxious about the boy. Finally I sank upon the bed at the farther end of the room, for my limbs were tired and weighted with a heavy oppression. I would rest for a moment, but nothing would induce me to close my eyes. So I thought, and flung myself back on my pillow. But the next instant all present things were forgotten in dreamless and heavy slumber.

I awoke long hours afterward, to find the sunshine flooding the room, the window which led on to the balcony wide open, and Cecil's bed empty. I sprang up with a cry; memory returned with a flash. What had happened? Had

Fietta managed to get in by means of the window? I had noticed the balcony outside the window on the previous night.
The balcony of the next room was but a few feet distant
from mine. It would be easy for any one to enter there,
spring from one balcony to the other, and so obtain access to
my room. Doubtless this had been done. Why had I slept? I
had firmly resolved to stay awake all night. In an instant I
had found the solution. Fietta's letter had been a trap. The
envelope which he sent me contained poison on the gum. I
had licked it, and so received the fatal soporific. My heart
beat wildly. I knew I had not an instant to lose. With hasty
strides I went into Fietta's sitting-room: there was no one
there; into his bedroom, the door of which was open: it was
also empty. I rushed into the hall.

"The gentleman and the little boy went out about half an
hour ago," said the concierge, in answer to my inquiries.
"They have gone to Vesuvius—a fine day for the trip." The
man smiled as he spoke.

My heart almost stopped.

"How did they go?" I asked.

"A carriage, two horses—best way to go."

In a second I was out in the Piazza del Municipio.
Hastily selecting a pair-horse carriage out of the group of
importunate drivers, I jumped in.

"Vesuvius," I shouted, "as hard as you can go."

The man began to bargain. I thrust a roll of paper-
money into his hand. On receiving it he waited no longer,
and we were soon dashing at a furious speed along the
crowded, ill-paved streets, scattering the pedestrians as we

went. Down the Via Roma, and out on to the Santa Lucia Quay, away and away through endless labyrinths of noisome, narrow streets, till at length we got out into the more open country at the base of the burning mountain. Should I be in time to prevent the catastrophe which I dreaded? For I had been up that mountain before, and knew well the horrible danger at the crater's mouth—a slip, a push, and one would never be seen again.

The ascent began, and the exhausted horses were beginning to fail. I leapt out, and giving the driver a sum which I did not wait to count, ran up the winding road of cinders and pumice that curves round beneath the observatory. My breath had failed me, and my heart was beating so hard that I could scarcely speak when I reached the station where one takes ponies to go over the new, rough lava. In answer to my inquiries, Cook's agent told me that Fietta and Cecil had gone on not a quarter of an hour ago.

I shouted my orders, and flinging money right and left, I soon obtained a fleet pony, and was galloping recklessly over the broken lava. Throwing the reins over the pony's head I presently jumped off, and ran up the little, narrow path to the funicular wire-laid railway that takes passengers up the steep cone to the crater.

"Just gone on, sir," said a Cook's official, in answer to my question.

"But I must follow at once," I said excitedly, hurrying toward the little shed.

The man stopped me.

"We don't take single passengers," he answered.

"I will, and must, go alone," I said. "I'll buy the car, and the railway, and you, and the mountain, if necessary, but go I will. How much do you want to take me alone?"

"One hundred francs," he answered impertinently, little thinking that I would agree to the bargain.

"Done!" I replied.

In astonishment he counted out the notes which I handed to him, and hurried at once into the shed. Here he rang an electric bell to have the car at the top started back, and getting into the empty car, I began to ascend—up, and up, and up. Soon I passed the empty car returning. How slowly we moved! My mouth was parched and dry, and I was in a fever of excitement. The smoke from the crater was close above me in great wreaths. At last we reached the top. I leapt out, and without waiting for a guide, made my way past, and rushed up the active cone, slipping in the shifting, loose, gritty soil. When I reached the top a gale was blowing, and the scenery below, with the Bay and Naples and Sorrento, lay before me the most magnificent panorama in the world. I had no time to glance at it, but hurried forward past crags of hot rock, from which steam and sulphur were escaping. The wind was taking the huge volumes of smoke over to the farther side of the crater, and I could just catch sight of two figures as the smoke cleared for a moment. The figures were those of Fietta and the boy. They were evidently making a detour of the crater, and had just entered the smoke. I heard a guide behind shout something to me in Italian, but I took no notice, and plunged at once into the blinding, suffocating smoke that came belching forth from the crater.

I was now close behind Fietta and the boy. They held their handkerchiefs up to their faces to keep off the choking sulphurous fumes, and had evidently not seen me. Their guide was ahead of them. Fietta was walking slowly; he was farthest away from the crater's mouth. The boy's hand was within his; the boy was nearest to the yawning gulf. A hot and choking blast of smoke blinded me for a moment, and hid the pair from view; the next instant it passed. I saw Fietta suddenly turn, seize the boy, and push him toward the edge. Through the rumbling thunder that came from below I heard a sharp cry of terror, and bounding forward I just caught the lad as he reeled, and hurled him away into safety.

With a yell of baffled rage Fietta dashed through the smoke and flung himself upon me. I moved nimbly aside, and the doctor, carried on by the impetus of his rush, missed his footing in the crumbling ashes and fell headlong down through the reeking smoke and steam into the fathomless, seething cauldron below.

What followed may be told in a few words. That evening I sailed for Malta with the boy. Dr. Benson administered the antitoxin in time, and the child's life was saved. Within a fortnight I brought him back to his mother.

It was reported that Dr. Fietta had gone mad at the edge of the crater, and in an excess of maniacal fury had first tried to destroy the boy and then flung himself in. I kept my secret.

THE
VIOLET CAR
E. Nesbit
(1858–1924)

EDITH NESBIT, the daughter of schoolmaster John
Collis Nesbit, attended school in both England and
France. At the young age of 19, she married Hubert
Bland, a writer with very firm political ideas. The
couple joined with a group of their friends to form
the Fabian Society, an organization that discussed
and promoted socialism. Many other famous social-
ists in London came to the meetings to support this
political movement. Nesbit devoted the early part
of her career to writing and lecturing on socialism.
Her taste in fashion was as unusual as her politics,
for she kept her hair short, smoked, and wore loose,
flowing clothes, unlike most women of her time.

Toward the end of the 1880s, Nesbit began spending less time on her political activities. She concen-
trated on writing children's books, including the
extremely popular *Five Children and It*, *The Story
of the Treasure-Seekers*, and *The Phoenix and the
Carpet*. Perhaps her most famous novel is *The Railway Children*, which tells the story of a family who
moves to the country after the father is unfairly arrested as a spy. In addition to her novels, Nesbit was

well respected for her short stories, many of which contained supernatural elements. In fact, the following story was the first to feature a ghost in the form of an automobile.

I am unaccustomed to literary effort—and I feel that I shall not say what I have to say, or that it will convince you, unless I say it very plainly. I thought I could adorn my story with pleasant words, prettily arranged. But as I pause to think of what really happened, I see that the plainest words will be the best. I do not know how to weave a plot, nor how to embroider it. It is best not to try. These things happened. I have no skill to add to what happened; nor is any adding of mine needed.

I am a nurse—and I was sent for to go to Charlestown —a mental case. It was November—and the fog was thick in London, so that my cab went at a foot's pace, so I missed the train by which I should have gone. I sent a telegram to Charlestown, and waited in the dismal waiting room at London Bridge. The time was passed for me by a little child. Its mother, a widow, seemed too crushed to be able to respond to its quick questionings. She answered briefly, and not, as it seemed, to the child's satisfaction. The child itself presently seemed to perceive that its mother was not, so to speak, available. It leaned back on the wide, dusty seat and yawned. I caught its eye, and smiled. It would not smile, but it looked. I took out of my bag a silk purse, bright with beads and steel tassels, and turned it over and over. Presently, the child slid along the seat and said, "Let me"— After that all was easy. The mother sat with eyes closed. When I rose to go, she opened them and thanked me. The child, clinging, kissed me. Later, I saw them get into a first-class carriage in my train. My ticket was a third-class one.

I expected, of course, that there would be a conveyance of some sort to meet me at the station—but there was nothing. Nor was there a cab or a fly to be seen. It was by this time nearly dark, and the wind was driving the rain almost horizontally along the unfrequented road that lay beyond the door of the station. I looked out, forlorn and perplexed.

"Haven't you engaged a carriage?" It was the widow lady who spoke.

I explained.

"My motor will be here directly," she said, "you'll let me drive you? Where is it you are going?"

"Charlestown," I said, and as I said it, I was aware of a very odd change in her face. A faint change, but quite unmistakable.

"Why do you look like that?" I asked her bluntly. And, of course, she said, "Like what?"

"There's nothing wrong with the house?" I said, for that, I found, was what I had taken that faint change to signify; and I was very young, and one has heard tales. "No reason why I shouldn't go there, I mean?"

"No—oh, no—" She glanced out through the rain, and I knew as well as though she had told me that there was a reason why she should not wish to go there.

"Don't trouble," I said, "it's very kind of you—but it's probably out of your way and . . ."

"Oh—but I'll take you—of *course* I'll take you," she said, and the child said, "Mother, here comes the car."

And come it did, though neither of us heard it till the child had spoken. I know nothing of motor cars, and I don't know the names of any of the parts of them. This was like a brougham—only you got in at the back, as you do in a wagonette; the seats were in the corners, and when the door was shut there was a little seat that pulled up, and the child sat on it between us. And it moved like magic—or like a dream of a train.

We drove quickly through the dark—I could hear the wind screaming, and the wild dashing of the rain against the windows, even through the whirring of the machinery. One could see nothing of the country—only the black night, and the shafts of light from the lamps in front.

After, as it seemed, a very long time, the chauffeur got down and opened a gate. We went through it, and after that the road was very much rougher. We were quite silent in the car, and the child had fallen asleep.

We stopped, and the car stood pulsating as though it were out of breath, while the chauffeur hauled down my box. It was so dark that I could not see the shape of the house, only the lights in the downstairs windows, and the low-walled front garden faintly revealed by their light and the light of the motor lamps. Yet I felt that it was a fair-sized house, that it was surrounded by big trees, and that there was a pond or river close by. In daylight next day I found that all this was so. I have never been able to tell how I knew it that first night, in the dark, but I did know it. Perhaps there was something in the way the rain fell on the trees and on the water. I don't know.

The chauffeur took my box up a stone path, whereon I got out, and said my good-byes and thanks.

"Don't wait, please, don't," I said. "I'm all right now. Thank you a thousand times!"

The car, however, stood pulsating till I had reached the doorstep, then it caught its breath, as it were, throbbed more loudly, turned, and went.

And still the door had not opened. I felt for the knocker, and rapped smartly. Inside the door I was sure I heard whispering. The car light was fast diminishing to a little distant star, and its panting sounded now hardly at all. When it ceased to sound at all, the place was quiet as death. The lights glowed redly from curtained windows, but there was no other sign of life. I wished I had not been in such a hurry to part from my escort, from human companionship, and from the great, solid, competent presence of the motor car.

I knocked again, and this time I followed the knock by a shout.

"Hello!" I cried. "Let me in. I'm the nurse!"

There was a pause, such a pause as would allow time for whisperers to exchange glances on the other side of a door.

Then a bolt ground back, a key turned, and the doorway framed no longer cold, wet wood, but light and a welcoming warmth—and faces.

"Come in, oh, come in," said a voice, a woman's voice, and the voice of a man said: "We didn't know there was anyone there."

209

And I had shaken the very door with my knockings!

I went in, blinking at the light, and the man called a servant, and between them they carried my box upstairs.

The woman took my arm and led me into a low, square room, pleasant, homely, and comfortable, with a solid mid-Victorian comfort—the kind that expressed itself in rep and mahogany. In the lamplight I turned to look at her. She was small and thin, her hair, her face, and her hands were of the same tint of grayish yellow.

"Mrs. Eldridge?" I asked.

"Yes," said she, very softly. "Oh! I am so glad you have come. I hope you won't be dull here. I hope you'll stay. I hope I shall be able to make you comfortable."

She had a gentle, urgent way of speaking that was very winning.

"I'm sure I shall be very comfortable," I said; "but it's I that am to take care of you. Have you been ill long?"

"It's not me that's ill, really," she said, "it's him—"

Now, it was Mr. Robert Eldridge who had written to engage me to attend on his wife, who was, he said, slightly deranged.

"I see," said I. One must never contradict them, it only aggravates their disorder.

"The reason . . ." she was beginning, when his foot sounded on the stairs, and she fluttered off to get candles and hot water.

He came in and shut the door. A fair, bearded, elderly man, quite ordinary.

"You'll take care of her," he said. "I don't want her to get talking to people. She fancies things."

"What form do the illusions take?" I asked, prosaically.

"She thinks I'm mad," he said, with a short laugh.

"It's a very usual form. Is that all?"

"It's about enough. And she can't hear things that I can hear, see things that I can see, and she can't smell things. By the way, you didn't see or hear anything of a motor as you came up, did you?"

"I came up *in* a motor car," I said shortly. "You never sent to meet me, and a lady gave me a lift." I was going to explain about my missing the earlier train, when I found that he was not listening to me. He was watching the door. When his wife came in, with a steaming jug in one hand and a flat candlestick in the other, he went toward her, and whispered eagerly. The only words I caught were: "She came in a real motor."

Apparently, to these simple people a motor was as great a novelty as to me. My telegram, by the way, was delivered next morning.

They were very kind to me; they treated me as an honored guest. When the rain stopped, as it did late the next day, and I was able to go out, I found that Charlestown was a farm, a large farm, but even to my inexperienced eyes, it seemed neglected and unprosperous. There was absolutely nothing for me to do but to follow Mrs. Eldridge, helping her where I could in her household duties, and to sit with her while she sewed in the homely parlor. When I had been in the house a few days, I began to put together the little things that I had noticed singly, and the life at the farm seemed suddenly to come into focus, as strange surroundings do after a while.

I found that I had noticed that Mr. and Mrs. Eldridge were very fond of each other, and that it was a fondness, and their way of showing it was a way that told that they had known sorrow, and had borne it together. That she showed no sign of mental derangement, save in the persistent belief of hers that he was deranged. That the morning found them fairly cheerful; that after the early dinner they seemed to grow more and more depressed; that after the "early cup of tea"—that is just as dusk was falling—they always went for a walk together. That they never asked me to join them in this walk, and that it always took the same direction—across the downs toward the sea. That they always returned from this walk pale and dejected; that she sometimes cried afterward alone in their bedroom, while he was shut up in the little room they called the office, where he did his accounts, and paid his men's wages, and where his hunting-crops and guns were kept. After supper, which was early, they always made an effort to be cheerful. I knew that this effort was for my sake, and I knew that each of them thought it was good for the other to make it.

Just as I had known before they showed it to me that Charlestown was surrounded by big trees and had a great pond beside it, so I knew, and in as inexplicable a way, that with these two fear lived. It looked at me out of their eyes. And I knew, too, that this was not her fear. I had not been two days in the place before I found that I was beginning to be fond of them both. They were so kind, so gentle, so ordinary, so homely—the kind of people who ought not to have known the name of fear—the kind of people to whom all honest, simple joys should have come by right, and no sorrows but such as come to us all, the death of old friends, and the slow changes of advancing years.

They seemed to belong to the land—to the downs, and the copses, and the old pastures, and the lessening cornfields. I found myself wishing that I, too, belonged to these, that I had been born a farmer's daughter. All the stress and struggle of cram and exam, of school, and college and hospital, seemed so loud and futile, compared with these open secrets of the down life. And I felt this the more, as more and more I felt that I must leave it all—that there was, honestly, no work for me here such as for good or ill I had been trained to do.

"I ought not to stay," I said to her one afternoon, as we stood at the open door. It was February now, and the snow-drops were thick in tufts beside the flagged path. "You are quite well."

"*I* am," she said.

"You are quite well, both of you," I said. "I oughtn't to be taking your money and doing nothing for it."

"You're doing everything," she said; "You don't know how much you're doing.

"We had a daughter of our own once," she added vaguely, and then, after a very long pause, she said very quietly and distinctly:

"He has never been the same since."

"How not the same?" I asked, turning my face up to the thin February sunshine.

She tapped her wrinkled, yellow-gray forehead, as country people do.

"Not right here," she said.

"How?" I asked. "Dear Mrs. Eldridge, tell me; perhaps I could help somehow."

Her voice was so sane, so sweet. It had come to this with me, that I did not know which of these two was the one who needed my help.

"He sees things that no one else sees, and hears things no one else hears, and smells things you can't smell if you're standing there beside him."

I remembered with a sudden smile his words to me on the morning of my arrival:

"She can't see, or hear, or smell."

And once more I wondered to which of the two I owed my service.

"Have you any idea why?" I asked. She caught at my arm.

"It was after our Bessie died," she said—"the very day she was buried. The motor that killed her—they said it was an accident—it was on the Brighton Road. It was a violet color. They go into mourning for Queens with violet, don't they?' she added; "and my Bessie, she was a Queen. So the motor was violet: That was all right, wasn't it?"

I told myself now that I saw that the woman was not normal, and I saw why. It was grief that had turned her brain. There must have been some change in my look, though I ought to have known better, for she said suddenly, "No. I'll not tell you any more."

And then he came out. He never left me alone with her for very long. Nor did she ever leave him for very long alone with me.

I did not intend to spy upon them, though I am not sure that my position as nurse to one mentally afflicted would not have justified such spying. But I did not spy. It was chance. I had been to the village to get some blue sewing silk for a blouse I was making, and there was a royal sunset which tempted me to prolong my walk. That was how I found myself on the high downs where they slope to the broken edge of England—the sheer, white cliffs against which the English Channel beats forever. The furze was in flower, and the skylarks were singing, and my thoughts were with my own life, my own hopes and dreams. So I found that I had struck a road, without knowing when I had struck it. I followed it toward the sea, and quite soon it ceased to be a road, and merged in the pathless turf as a stream sometimes disappears in sand. There was nothing but turf and furze bushes, the song of the skylarks, and beyond the slope that ended at the cliff's edge, the booming of the sea. I turned back, following the road, which defined itself again a few yards back, and presently sank to a lane, deep-banked and bordered with brown hedge stuff. It was there that I came upon them in the dusk. And I heard their voices before I saw them, and before it was possible for them to see me. It was her voice that I heard first.

"No, no, no, no, no," it said.

"I tell you yes," that was his voice; "there—can't you hear it, that panting sound—right away—away? It must be at the very edge of the cliff."

"There's nothing, dearie," she said, "indeed there's nothing."

"You're deaf—and blind—stand back I tell you, it's close upon us."

I came round the corner of the lane then, and as I came,

I saw him catch her arm and throw her against the hedge—violently, as though the danger he feared were indeed close upon them. I stopped behind the turn of the hedge and stepped back. They had not seen me. Her eyes were on his face, and they held a world of pity, love, agony—his face was set in a mask of terror, and his eyes moved quickly as though they followed down the lane the swift passage of something—something that neither she nor I could see. Next moment he was cowering, pressing his body into the hedge—his face hidden in his hands, and his whole body trembling so that I could see it, even from where I was a dozen yards away, through the light screen of the overgrown hedge.

"And the smell of it!"—he said, "do you mean to tell me you can't smell it?"

She had her arms round him.

"Come home, dearie," she said. "Come home! It's all your fancy—come home with your old wife that loves you."

They went home.

Next day I asked her to come to my room to look at the new blue blouse. When I had shown it to her, I told her what I had seen and heard yesterday in the lane.

"And now I know," I said, "which of you it is that wants care."

To my amazement she said very eagerly, "Which?"

"Why, he—of course"—I told her, "there was nothing there."

She sat down in the chintz covered armchair by the window, and broke into wild weeping. I stood by her and soothed her as well as I could.

"It's a comfort to know," she said at last. "I haven't known what to believe. Many a time, lately, I've wondered whether after all it could be me that was mad, like he said. And there was nothing there? There always was nothing there—and it's on him the judgment, not on me. On him. Well, that's something to be thankful for."

So her tears, I told myself, had been more of relief at her own escape. I looked at her with distaste, and forgot that I had been fond of her. So that her next words cut me like little knives.

"It's bad enough for him as it is," she said, "but it's nothing to what it would be for him, if I was really to go off my head and him left to think he'd brought it on me. You see, now I can look after him the same as I've always done. It's only once in the day it comes over him. He couldn't bear it, if it was all the time—like it'll be for me now. It's much better it should be him—I'm better able to bear it than he is."

I kissed her then and put my arms round her, and said, "Tell me what it is that frightens him so—and it's every day, you say?"

"Yes—ever since . . . I'll tell you. It's a sort of comfort to speak out. It was a violet-colored car that killed our Bessie. You know our girl that I've told you about. And it's a violet-colored car that he thinks he sees—every day up there in the lane. And he says he hears it, and that he smells the smell of the machinery—the stuff they put in it—you know."

"Petrol?"

"Yes, and you can *see* he hears it, and you can see he sees it. It haunts him, as if it was a ghost. You see, it was he that picked her up after the violet car went over her. It was that that turned him. I only saw her as he carried her in, in his arms—and then he'd covered her face. But he saw her just as they'd left her, lying in the dust . . . you could see the place on the road where it happened for days and days."

"Didn't they come back?"

"Oh, yes . . . they came back. But Bessie didn't come back. But there was a judgment on them. The very night of the funeral, that violet car went over the cliff—dashed to pieces—every soul in it. That was the man's widow that drove you home the first night."

"I wonder she uses a car after that," I said—I wanted something commonplace to say.

"Oh," said Mrs. Eldridge, "it's all what you're used to. We don't stop walking because our girl was killed on the road. Motoring comes as natural to them as walking to us. There's my old man calling—poor old dear. He wants me to go out with him."

She went, all in a hurry, and in her hurry slipped on the stairs and twisted her ankle. It all happened in a minute and it was a bad sprain.

When I had bound it up, and she was on the sofa, she looked at him, standing as if he were undecided, staring out of the window, with his cap in his hand. And she looked at me.

"Mr. Eldridge mustn't miss his walk," she said. "You go with him, my dear. A breath of air will do you good."

So I went, understanding as well as though he had told me, that he did not want me with him, and that he was afraid to go alone, and that he yet had to go.

We went up the lane in silence. At that corner he stopped suddenly, caught my arm, and dragged me back. His eyes followed something that I could not see. Then he exhaled a held breath, and said, "I thought I heard a motor coming." He had found it hard to control his terror, and I saw beads of sweat on his forehead and temples. Then we went back to the house.

The sprain was a bad one. Mrs. Eldridge had to rest, and again next day it was I who went with him to the corner of the lane.

This time he could not, or did not try to, conceal what he felt. "There—listen!" he said. "Surely you can hear it?"

I heard nothing.

"Stand back," he cried shrilly, suddenly, and we stood back close against the hedge.

Again the eyes followed something invisible to me, and again the held breath exhaled.

"It will kill me one of these days," he said, "and I don't know that I care how soon—if it wasn't for her."

"Tell me," I said, full of that importance, that conscious competence, that one feels in the presence of other people's troubles. He looked at me.

"I will tell you, by God," he said. "I couldn't tell *her*. Young lady, I've gone so far as wishing myself a Roman, for the sake of a priest to tell it to. But I can tell *you*, without losing my soul more than it's lost already. Did you ever hear tell of a violet car that got smashed up—went over the cliff?"

"Yes," I said. "Yes."

"The man that killed my girl was new to the place. And

he hadn't any eyes—or ears—or he'd have known me, seeing we'd been face to face at the inquest. And you'd have thought he'd have stayed at home that one day, with the blinds drawn down. But not he. He was swirling and swivelling all about the country in his cursed violet car, the very time we were burying her. And at dusk—there was a mist coming up—he comes up behind me in this very lane, and I stood back, and he pulls up, and he calls out, with his damned lights full in my face: 'Can you tell me the way to Hexham, my man?' says he.

"I'd have liked to show him the way to hell. And that was the way for me, not him. I don't know how I came to do it. I didn't mean to do it. I didn't think I was going to—and before I knew anything, I'd said it. 'Straight ahead,' I said; 'keep straight ahead.' Then the motor-thing panted, chuckled, and he was off. I ran after him to try to stop him—but what's the use of running after these motor-devils? And he kept straight on. And every day since then, every dear day, the car comes by, the violet car that nobody can see but me—and it keeps straight on."

"You ought to go away," I said, speaking as I had been trained to speak. "You fancy these things. You probably fancied the whole thing. I don't suppose you ever did tell the violet car to go straight ahead. I expect it was all imagination, and the shock of your poor daughter's death. You ought to go right away."

"I can't," he said earnestly. "If I did, someone else would see the car. You see, somebody *has* to see it every day as long as I live. If it wasn't me, it would be someone else. And I'm the only person who *deserves* to see it. I wouldn't like anyone else to see it—it's too horrible. *It's* much more horrible than you think," he added slowly.

I asked him, walking beside him down the quiet lane, what it was that was so horrible about the violet car. I think I quite expected him to say that it was splashed with his daughter's blood . . . What he did say was, "It's too horrible to tell you," and he shuddered.

I was young then, and youth always thinks it can move mountains. I persuaded myself that I could cure him of his delusion by attacking—not the main fort—that is always, to begin with, impregnable, but one, so to speak, of the out-works. I set myself to persuade him not to go to that corner in the lane, at that hour in the afternoon.

"But if I don't, someone else will see it."

"There'll be nobody there *to* see it," I said briskly.

"Someone will be there. Mark my words, someone will be there—and then they'll know."

"Then I'll be the someone," I said. "Come—you stay at home with your wife, and *I'll* go—and if I see it I'll promise to tell you, and if I don't—well, then I will be able to go away with a clear conscience."

"A clear conscience," he repeated.

I argued with him in every moment when it was possible to catch him alone. I put all my will and all my energy into my persuasions. Suddenly, like a door that you've been trying to open, and that has resisted every key till the last one, he gave way. Yes—I should go to the lane. And he would not go.

I went.

Being, as I said before, a novice in the writing of stories, I perhaps haven't made you understand that it was quite hard for me to go—that I felt myself at once a coward and a heroine. This business of an imaginary motor that only one poor old farmer could see, probably appears to you quite commonplace and ordinary. It was not so with me. You see, the idea of this thing had dominated my life for weeks and months, and had dominated it even before I knew the nature of the domination. It was this that was the fear that I had known to walk with these two people, the fear that shared their bed and board, that lay down and rose up with them. The old man's fear of this and his fear of his fear. And the old man was terribly convincing. When one talked with him, it was quite difficult to believe that he was mad, and that there wasn't, and couldn't be, a mysteriously horrible motor that was visible to him, and invisible to other people. And when he said that, if he were not in the lane, someone else would see it—it was easy to say "Nonsense," but to think "Nonsense" was not so easy, and to *feel* "Nonsense" quite oddly difficult.

I walked up and down the lane in the dusk, wishing not to wonder what might be the hidden horror in the violet car. I would not let blood into my thoughts. I was not going to be fooled by thought transference, or any of those transcendental follies. I was not going to be hypnotized into seeing things.

I walked up the lane—I had promised him to stand at the corner for five minutes, and I stood there in the deepening dusk, looking up toward the downs and the sea. There were pale stars. Everything was very still. Five minutes is a long time. I held my watch in my hand. Four—four and a quarter—four and a half. Five. I turned instantly. And then I saw that *he* had followed me—he was standing a dozen

yards away—and his face was turned from me. It was turned toward a motor car that shot up the lane. It came very swiftly, and before it came to where he was, I knew that it was very horrible. I crushed myself back into the crackling bare hedge, as I should have done to leave room for the passage of a real car—though I knew that this one was not real. It looked real—but I knew it was not.

As it neared him, he started back, then suddenly he cried out. I heard him. "No, no, no, no—no more, no more," was what he cried, with that he flung himself down on the road in front of the car, and its great tires passed over him. Then the car shot past me and I saw what the full horror of it was. There was no blood—that was not the horror. The color of it was, as she had said, violet.

I got to him and got his head up. He was dead. I was quite calm and collected now, and felt that to be so was extremely creditable to me. I went to a cottage where a laborer was having tea—he got some men and a hurdle.

When I had told his wife, the first intelligible thing she said was: "It's better for him. Whatever he did he's paid for now" So it looks as though she had known—or guessed—more than he thought.

I stayed with her till her death. She did not live long.

You think perhaps that the old man was knocked down and killed by a real motor, which happened to come that way of all ways, at that hour of all hours, and happened to be, of all colors, violet. Well, a real motor leaves its mark on you where it kills you, doesn't it? But when I lifted up that old man's head from the road, there was no mark on him, no blood—no broken bones—his hair was not disordered, nor his dress. I tell you there was not even a speck of mud on him, except where he had touched the road in falling. There were no tire-marks in the mud.

The motor car that killed him came and went like a shadow. As he threw himself down, it swerved a little so that both its wheels should go over him.

He died, the doctor said, of heart failure. I am the only person to know that he was killed by a violet car, which, having killed him, went noiselessly away toward the sea. And that car was empty—there was no one in it. It was just a violet car that moved along the lanes swiftly and silently, and was empty.

GABRIEL-ERNEST

Saki
(1870–1916)

SAKI, whose real name was Hector Hugh Munro, was born in Burma to Scottish parents. Sadly, Munro's mother died when he was young, so he and his brothers and sisters were sent to England to live with their aunts. According to Munro's sister, their Aunt Augusta was "a woman of ungovernable temper . . . possessing no brains worth speaking of." Although the two ladies made Munro's life miserable, he got his revenge by writing tale after frightening tale about stupid or tyrannical aunts who are fooled by cunning children. The child in this story, Gabriel-Ernest, would certainly cause even the fiercest aunt trouble, at least after dark.

H. H. Munro chose his odd pen-name from *The Rubáiyát*, a poem written by Omar Khayyám, a poet and astronomer from the eleventh century. Using the name Saki, Munro gained popularity as a writer of amusing political sketches and humorous short stories. Many of Munro's stories are eerie if not a little frightening. Unfortunately, Munro died at the young age of 46, while fighting in France during World War I. He had not quite recovered from a

bout of malaria, but insisted on leaving the hospital and returning to his battalion, He was killed by a sniper in the early hours of a winter's dawn on November 13, 1916.

There is a wild beast in your woods," said the artist Cunningham, as he was being driven to the station. It was the only remark he had made during the drive, but as Van Cheele had talked incessantly his companion's silence had not been noticeable.

"A stray fox or two and some resident weasels. Nothing more formidable," said Van Cheele. The artist said nothing.

"What did you mean about a wild beast?" said Van Cheele later, when they were on the platform.

"Nothing. My imagination. Here is the train," said Cunningham.

That afternoon Van Cheele went for one of his frequent rambles through his woodland property. He had a stuffed bittern in his study, and knew the names of quite a number of wild flowers, so his aunt had possibly some justification in describing him as a great naturalist. At any rate, he was a great walker. It was his custom to take mental notes of everything he saw during his walks, not so much for the purpose of assisting contemporary science as to provide topics for conversation afterwards. When the bluebells began to show themselves in flower he made a point of informing every one of the fact; the season of the year might have warned his hearers of the likelihood of such an occurrence, but at least they felt that he was being absolutely frank with them.

What Van Cheele saw on this particular afternoon was, however, something far removed from his ordinary range of experience. On a shelf of smooth stone overhanging a deep pool in the hollow of an oak coppice a boy of about sixteen lay asprawl, drying his wet brown limbs luxuriously in the sun. His wet hair, parted by a recent dive, lay close to his head, and his light-brown eyes, so light that there was an almost tigerish gleam in them, were turned towards Van Cheele with a certain lazy watchfulness. It was an unexpected apparition, and Van Cheele found himself engaged in the novel process of thinking before he spoke. Where on earth could this wild-looking boy hail from? The miller's wife had lost a child some two months ago, supposed to have been swept away by the mill-race, but that had been a mere baby, not a half-grown lad.

"What are you doing there?" he demanded.

"Obviously, sunning myself," replied the boy.

"Where do you live?"

"Here, in these woods."

"You can't live in the woods," said Van Cheele.

"They are very nice woods," said the boy, with a touch of patronage in his voice.

"But where do you sleep at night?"

"I don't sleep at night; that's my busiest time."

Van Cheele began to have an irritated feeling that he was grappling with a problem that was eluding him.

"What do you feed on?" he asked.

"Flesh," said the boy, and he pronounced the word with slow relish, as though he were tasting it.

"Flesh! What flesh?"

"Since it interests you, rabbits, wild-fowl, hares, poultry, lambs in their season, children when I can get any; they're usually too well locked in at night, when I do most of my hunting. It's quite two months since I tasted child-flesh."

Ignoring the chaffing nature of the last remark Van Cheele tried to draw the boy on the subject of possible poaching operations.

"You're talking rather through your hat when you speak of feeding on hares." (Considering the nature of the boys toilet the simile was hardly an apt one.) "Our hillside hares aren't easily caught."

"At night I hunt on four feet," was the somewhat cryptic response.

"I suppose you mean that you hunt with a dog?" hazarded Van Cheele.

The boy rolled slowly over on to his back, and laughed a weird low laugh, that was pleasantly like a chuckle and disagreeably like a snarl.

"I don't fancy any dog would be very anxious for my company, especially at night."

Van Cheele began to feel that there was something positively uncanny about the strange-eyed, strange-tongued youngster.

"I can't have you staying in these woods," he declared authoritatively.

"I fancy you'd rather have me here than in your house," said the boy.

The prospect of this wild, nude animal in Van Cheele's primly ordered house was certainly an alarming one.

"If you don't go I shall have to make you," said Van Cheele.

The boy turned like a flash, plunged into the pool, and in a moment had flung his wet and glistening body half-way up the bank where Van Cheele was standing. In an otter the movement would not have been remarkable; in a boy Van Cheele found it sufficiently startling. His foot slipped as he made an involuntary backward movement, and he found himself almost prostrate on the slippery weed-grown bank, with those tigerish yellow eyes not very far from his own. Almost instinctively he half raised his hand to his throat. The boy laughed again, a laugh in which the snarl had nearly driven out the chuckle, and then, with another of his astonishing lightning movements, plunged out of view into a yielding tangle of weed and fern.

"What an extraordinary wild animal?" said Van Cheele as he picked himself up. And then he recalled Cunningham's remark, "There is a wild beast in your woods."

Walking slowly homeward, Van Cheele began to turn over in his mind various local occurrences which might be traceable to the existence of this astonishing young savage.

Something had been thinning the game in the woods lately, poultry had been missing from the farms, hares were growing unaccountably scarcer, and complaints had reached him of lambs being carried off bodily from the hills. Was it possible that this wild boy was really hunting the countryside in company with some clever poacher dog? He had spoken of hunting "four-footed" by night, but then, again, he had hinted strangely at no dog caring to come near him, "especially at night." It was certainly puzzling. And then, as Van Cheele ran his mind over the various depredations that had been committed during the last month or two, he came suddenly to a dead stop, alike in his walk and his speculations. The child missing from the mill two months ago—the accepted theory was that it had tumbled into the mill-race and been swept away; but the mother had always declared she had heard a shriek on the hill side of the house, in the opposite direction from the water. It was unthinkable, of course, but he wished that the boy had not made that uncanny remark about child-flesh eaten two months ago. Such dreadful things should not be said even in fun.

Van Cheele, contrary to his usual wont, did not feel disposed to be communicative about his discovery in the wood. His position as a parish councilor and justice of the peace seemed somehow compromised by the fact that he was harboring a personality of such doubtful repute on his property; there was even a possibility that a heavy bill of damages for raided lambs and poultry might be laid at his door. At dinner that night he was quite unusually silent.

"Where's your voice gone to?" said his aunt. "One would think you had seen a wolf."

Van Cheele, who was not familiar with the old saying, thought the remark rather foolish; if he *had* seen a wolf on his property his tongue would have been extraordinarily busy with the subject.

At breakfast next morning Van Cheele was conscious that his feeling of uneasiness regarding yesterday's episode had not wholly disappeared, and he resolved to go by train to the neighboring cathedral town, hunt up Cunningham, and learn

from him what he had really seen that prompted the remark
about a wild beast in the woods. With this resolution taken, his
usual cheerfulness partially returned, and he hummed a bright
little melody as he sauntered to the morning room for his cus-
tomary cigarette. As he entered the room the melody made
way abruptly for a pious invocation. Gracefully asprawl on the
ottoman, in an attitude of almost exaggerated repose, was the
boy of the woods. He was drier than when V had last seen him,
but no other alteration was noticeable in his toilet.

"How dare you come here?" asked Van Cheele furiously.

"You told me I was not to stay in the woods," said the
boy calmly.

"But not to come here. Supposing my aunt should see
you?"

And with a view to minimizing that catastrophe Van
Cheele hastily obscured as much of his unwelcome guest as
possible under the folds of a *Morning Post*. At that moment
his aunt entered the room.

"This is a poor boy who has lost his way—and lost his
memory. He doesn't know who he is or where he comes
from," explained Van Cheele desperately, glancing appre-
hensively at the waif's face to see whether he was going to
add inconvenient candor to his other savage propensities.

Miss Van Cheele was enormously interested.

"Perhaps his underlinen is marked," she suggested.

"He seems to have lost most of that, too," said Van
Cheele, making frantic little grabs at the *Morning Post* to
keep it in its place.

A naked homeless child appealed to Miss Van Cheele as
warmly as a stray kitten or derelict puppy would have done.

"We must do all we can for him," she decided, and in a very short time a messenger, dispatched to the rectory, where a page-boy was kept, had returned with a suit of pantry clothes, and the necessary accessories of shirt, shoes, collar, etc. Clothed, clean, and groomed, the boy lost none of his uncanniness in Van Cheele's eyes, but his aunt found him sweet.

"We must call him something till we know who he really is," she said. "Gabriel-Ernest, I think; those are nice suitable names."

Van Cheele agreed, but he privately doubted whether they were being grafted on to a nice suitable child. His misgivings were not diminished by the fact that his staid and elderly spaniel had bolted out of the house at the first incoming of the boy, and now obstinately remained shivering and yapping at the farther end of the orchard, while the canary, usually as vocally industrious as Van Cheele himself, had put itself on an allowance of frightened cheeps. More than ever he was resolved to consult Cunningham without loss of time.

As he drove off to the station his aunt was arranging that Gabriel-Ernest should help her to entertain the infant members of her Sunday-school class at tea that afternoon.

Cunningham was not at first disposed to be communicative.

"My mother died of some brain trouble," he explained, "so you will understand why I am averse to dwelling on anything of an impossibly fantastic nature that I may see or think that I have seen."

"But what *did* you see?" persisted Van Cheele.

"What I thought I saw was something so extraordinary that no really sane man could dignify it with the credit of having actually happened. I was standing, the last evening I was with you, half-hidden in the hedgegrowth by the orchard gate, watching the dying glow of the sunset. Suddenly I became aware of a naked boy, a bather from some neighborhood pool, I took him to be, who was standing out on the bare hillside also watching the sunset. His pose was so suggestive of some wild faun of Pagan myth that I instantly wanted to engage him as a model, and in another moment I think I should have hailed him. But just then the sun dipped out of view, and all the orange and pink slid out of the landscape, leaving it cold and gray. And at the same moment an astounding thing happened—the boy vanished too!"

"What! vanished away into nothing?" asked Van Cheele excitedly.

"No; that is the dreadful part of it," answered the artist; "on the open hillside where the boy had been standing a second ago, stood a large wolf, blackish in color, with gleaming fangs and cruel, yellow eyes. You may think—"

But Van Cheele did not stop for anything as futile as thought. Already he was tearing at top speed towards the station. He dismissed the idea of a telegram. "Gabriel-Ernest is a werewolf" was a hopelessly inadequate effort at conveying the situation, and his aunt would think it was a code message to which he had omitted to give her the key. His one hope was that he might reach home before sundown. The cab which he chartered at the other end of the railway journey bore him with what seemed exasperating slowness along the country roads, which were pink and mauve with the flush of the sinking sun. His aunt was putting away some unfinished jams and cake when he arrived.

"Where is Gabriel-Ernest?" he almost screamed.

"He is taking the little Toop child home," said his aunt. "It was getting so late, I thought it wasn't safe to let it go back alone. What a lovely sunset, isn't it?"

But Van Cheele, although not oblivious of the glow in the western sky, did not stay to discuss its beauties. At a speed for which he was scarcely geared he raced along the narrow lane that led to the home of the Toops. On one side ran the swift current of the mill-stream, on the other rose the stretch of sky-line, and the next turning must bring him in view of the ill-assorted couple he was pursuing. Then the color went suddenly out of things, and a gray light settled itself with a quick shiver over the landscape. Van Cheele heard a shrill wail of fear, and stopped running.

Nothing was ever seen again of the Toop child or Gabriel-Ernest, but the latter's discarded garments were found lying in the road, so it was assumed that the child had fallen into the water, and that the boy had stripped and jumped in, in a vain endeavor to save it. Van Cheele and some workmen who were near by at the time testified to having heard a child scream loudly just near the spot where the clothes were found. Mrs. Toop, who had eleven other children, was decently resigned to her bereavement, but Miss Van Cheele sincerely mourned her lost foundling. It was on her initiative that a memorial brass was put up in the parish church to "Gabriel-Ernest, an unknown boy, who bravely sacrificed his life for another."

Van Cheele gave way to his aunt in most things, but he flatly refused to subscribe to the Gabriel-Ernest memorial.

GLOSSARY

THE LION

admonitions warnings or scoldings

anthropoids animals shaped like humans, usually apes

carnivora a class of animals who eat mainly meat,
    including lions, tigers, wolves, etc.

chastened ashamed, taught a lesson

craniums skulls

despoilers those who ruin a plan

eddied swirled in a circle

herbivora a class of animals who eat mainly plants,
    including zebras and deer

morose gloomy, sad, or cross

peevish bad tempered, fretful, or resentful

progenitor an ancestor

propensity a preference or liking

spoor the trail, scent, or droppings of a wild animal

temerity daring or boldness

timorous timid or fearful

undulating waving back and forth

wroth very angry

THE RED-HEADED LEAGUE

abutted was next to, touched

benefactor one who gives help, a good-deed doer

billet job, position; originally referred to a soldier's assignment

chagrin embarrassment, shame

cobblers' wax an old-fashioned type of shoe polish; might be used as hair dye by men desperate to join the Red-headed League

conundrums complex problems, puzzles

coster a fruit seller who displays produce in a wheel barrow; a collection of red-headed men might look like the oranges in his cart

engaged busy, involved in some task

florid-faced red-faced or blushing

Freemason a member of a club, the Freemasons, which originated as an organization of independent stoneworkers in the middle ages; symbolized by the arc and the compass, tools of the mason's trade

gilt gold covered; 3 gold balls marked a pawnbroker's shop

hansom a two-wheeled carriage

introspective thoughtful, reflective, contemplative

L'homme c'est rien—l'oeuvre c'est tout a French phrase meaning "The man is nothing—the work is all"

Omne ignotum pro magnifico a Latin motto meaning "All is unknown before explanation"

portly having a large stature, fat

recommence begin again, continue

settee a small sofa

solicitor a lawyer

snuff a type of tobacco which could be sniffed, popular at the time

waistcoat a vest of the type usually worn with a suit

THE ABSENCE OF MR. GLASS

clerical about or belonging to a priest

criminologist one who studies crime, an expert at catching criminals

dado a simple molding decorating the lower half of an interior wall

dissipation wasteful spending often combined with excessive gambling or drinking

eminent famous, well-respected

Kew Gardens a famous botanical garden in London, England

parochial about or belonging to a small church or its congregation

physiologist a doctor

prosaic everyday, ordinary, dull

querulous fretful or whining

reiterations repetitions of a speech

sanguine confident, cheerful, optimistic

serried crowded or pressed together

tantalus a small chest with visible containers of liquid that cannot be reached without a key

GOOD LADY DUCAYNE

anemic without much energy; technically, a disease in which the patient has too little iron in theblood or too little blood altogether

aristocracy families with high social positions, titles, and generally large bank accounts

chloroform a colorless liquid with a strong odor which produces unconsciousness when inhaled

eccentric mildly strange, unusual, or odd

florin a foreign coin with no value in England

lassitude exhaustion

Louis XVI king of France from 1774–1793, executed by guillotine in January, 1793 during the French Revolution

mantle a loose, sleeveless cloak worn over other clothes

querulous fretful or complaining

raiment clothing

vivacity liveliness or energy

THE STORY OF THE GOBLINS WHO STOLE A SEXTON

contemptuous scornful or disdainful

envious jealous

frugal poor, simple, designed to save money

gall and wormwood bitter-tasting medicine

malice evil or cruel intentions

morose gloomy, sad, or cross

pliable easily bent

sexton an employee of the church who takes care of the property, rings the bell, and digs graves

THE CANTERVILLE GHOST

amazon an ancient tribe of female warriors noted for their strength and independence

aristocracy families with high social positions, titles, and generally large bank accounts

arquebus a heavy, but portable gun invented in the fifteenth century

dogmatic opinionated, often reluctant to consider other
     points of view
falchion a wide, curved sword used in medieval times
impresarios managers or directors of entertainment
     companies such as operas, circuses, etc.
materialism a belief that *things* are more important
     than *emotions* or *ideas*
phantasmata ghosts, spirits, or their effects on the
     environment
punctilious careful and precise, worried about the
     proper way to do things
rector a pastor in charge of a small church
sanguineous having to do with blood
vulgarity rudeness or inappropriate behavior
wainscoting wooden boards lining the lower half of
     a wall

A RAID ON THE OYSTER PIRATES

aft towards the stern (or back of a boat)
ballast weights which give a boat stability in the water,
     or the place in the bottom of the boat that holds
     these weights
bowsprit a spar (or pole) extending from the mast to
     which the foresail is attached
centerboard the beam which runs along the bottom
     center of a boat, the keel
comprised made up, were included in
ebb receding tide
fore towards the bow (or front of a boat)

greenhorns amateurs, inexperienced first-timers

lubbery awkward handling of a ship due to inexperi-
ence, based on the term "land lubber," which sailors
called people who lived on land

natty neat, well-designed, dapper

rigging all the ropes and pulleys which support and
operate the sails

shoals a shallow sand bar

skiff a small, light sailing ship

slack water low tide, the moment when the tide begins
to turn

sloop a small ship with one mast that carries sails both
fore and aft

AT THE EDGE OF THE CRATER

antitoxin an antidote or cure for poison

bona fide true, guaranteed, without fraud; Latin for
"in good faith"

concierge a hotel employee who works near the
entrance, usually assisting visitors with directions,
restaurant reservations, etc.

efficacious effective

emissary someone sent on an errand, an agent

funicular shaped like a rope

guile cunning

hansom a two-wheeled carriage

importunate demanding or troublesome

impregnable secrecy unbreakable secrecy, extremely
confidential

malevolent dangerous, intimidating, forbidding

morphia a pain killer derived from morphine, may be addictive

pell-mell confused haste

physiology the science dealing with the structure and function of living organisms

pince-nez eyeglasses which rest on the nose but have no ear pieces

portmanteau a suitcase or trunk

recluse someone who lives alone and apart from society

salver tray or platter, often made of silver

savant a wise person, usually very well educated

scrupulousness careful attention to detail, acting in the proper way

soporific a substance causing drowsiness or sleep

THE VIOLET CAR

adorn decorate, embellish, or beautify

brougham a medium-sized carriage with the driver's seat in front

chintz printed cotton fabric

conveyance any type of vehicle such as an automobile, cart, or carriage

derangement confusion or mental illness

dismal dull or gloomy

fly a small carriage with room for 1–2 passengers

forlorn sad and a little lonely

futile useless

hunting-crops small whips used in horseback riding

inquest a formal investigation into the cause of death

mahogany a dark wood with a reddish color

perplexed confused

petrol fuel for automobile engines, gasoline

pulsating beating or vibrating rhythmically

rep a plain-weave fabric with noticeable crosswise ribs, probably something like corduroy

unfrequented rarely used, empty

GABRIEL-ERNEST

asprawl sprawling, spread out on the ground

bittern a type of bird, a heron

candor honesty, truthfulness

coppice a small group of trees

cryptic brief or short, not very helpful

formidable frightening or intimidating

incessantly without stopping

industrious busy

memorial brass a plaque honoring someone who has died

mill-race a fast moving stream which turns a mill wheel

naturalist one who is interested in nature and studies biology

pious invocation a religious prayer; in this case, Van Cheele probably said "Oh, my God!"

poaching the crime of hunting animals on someone else's property

propensities preferences or habits